Cedar River Daydreams

Other Books by Judy Baer

Second Chance
Judy Baer

BETHANY HOUSE PUBLISHERS
MINNEAPOLIS, MINNESOTA 55438

All Scripture quotations are taken from *The Everyday Bible, New Century Version*, copyright © 1987, 1988 by Word Publishing, Dallas, Texas 75039. Used by permission.

Cover illustration by Brett Longley, Bethany House Publishers staff artist.

Second Chance
Judy Baer

Library of Congress Catalog Card Number 91–72558

ISBN 1–55661–217–6

Published by Bethany House Publishers
A Ministry of Bethany Fellowship, Inc.
6820 Auto Club Road, Minneapolis, Minnesota 55438

Printed in the United States of America

For Christina Carroll:

Never give up hope.

JUDY BAER received a B.A. in English and Education from Concordia College in Moorhead, Minnesota. She has had over nineteen novels published and is a member of the National Romance Writers of America, the Society of Children's Book Writers and the National Federation of Press Women.

Two of her novels, *Adrienne* and *Paige*, have been prizewinning bestsellers in the Bethany House SPRINGFLOWER SERIES (for girls 12–15). Both books have been awarded first place for juvenile fiction in the National Federation of Press Women's communications contest.

"We know that in everything
God works for the good
of those who love him."

Romans 8:28a

Chapter One

"You'd better go home now, Lexi. I've called your parents."

Mrs. Winston entered the hospital's family waiting room and placed a comforting hand on Lexi's shoulder. Lexi Leighton bolted upright. She blinked her eyes and shook her head in an effort to remember where she was and why she had come.

Then with blinding clarity, she recalled the accident that had brought her here . . .

Saturday night had been a beautiful night for a football game. Todd Winston had begun to make a name for himself as Cedar River's finest quarterback. Everything had been perfect. Then Lexi's world fell apart.

She was sitting in the Cedar River stadium bleachers when her boyfriend and best friend, Todd Winston, was tackled and lay motionless beneath half a dozen opposing team members. With frustrating slowness the reality sank in—Todd was not going to get up on his own.

While Lexi stood frozen in time and space, the ambulance crew loaded Todd into the vehicle for the trip to the hospital. When she finally gained the pres-

ence of mind to go to him, it was too late. Her class-
mate, Minda Hannaford, drove her to the hospital.
Now, hours later, they were still awaiting word of
Todd's condition.

Lexi searched for hope in Mrs. Winston's eyes.

Ordinarily an attractive, confident woman, tonight Mrs. Winston looked like she'd aged ten years.
Her makeup was gone and she appeared exhausted
and fearful.

She had attended the game directly from work,
and still wore a business suit. Now she removed her
jacket and tried to smooth the skirt that was covered
with grass stains.

The family waiting room was less than cheerful.
It was painted a pale green, and the pictures on the
walls hung askew. There were sectional sofas along
two sides of the room and two shorter couches back-
to-back in the center. A writing table was cluttered
with newspapers, magazines and styrofoam cups.

Egg and Binky McNaughton were asleep on a
sofa. Egg, who was tall and skinny, dangled his feet
over one end of the couch. His sister, Binky, was
curled into a ball at the other end. Jennifer Golden
slept fitfully across from them.

"Is Todd any better?" Lexi asked, her voice plead-
ing.

Mrs. Winston shook her head and pursed her lips.
"We don't have any firm diagnosis yet. The doctors
are still conferring. We won't know for a while, and
it's getting quite late, Lexi."

"What time is it?" Lexi asked.

"After midnight. You'd better go home. There's
nothing you can do here."

"We can't leave now!" Lexi protested. "I want Todd to know we're here for him."

None of them had even gotten a glimpse of Todd since they arrived hours ago.

"That's very kind of you, Lexi, but it's going to be some time yet before you can see him." Despite her brave front, Mrs. Winston's voice trembled.

"Where's Mr. Winston?" Lexi wondered aloud, trying to choke back her panic.

"He and Todd's brother Mike needed some fresh air and went to the cafe down the street for coffee," Mrs. Winston explained.

"I wish there was something we could do. We've all prayed together. Maybe that's all we can do for now," Lexi said, staring at the floor.

"I think you're right." Mrs. Winston smiled at Lexi fondly. "I really do appreciate your prayers, and the concern and love you have all shown for Todd. It's comforting to Mr. Winston and me."

"You know we'll do anything we can to help."

"I know that, dear, but right now we just have to wait."

"Do you think Todd is seriously hurt?" Lexi questioned, afraid of the answer. "Why couldn't they have diagnosed his condition by now?"

"I suppose I can't keep what we know from you forever," Mrs. Winston said frankly.

Lexi felt a chill of fear wash over her. Her hands began to tremble and her mouth went dry.

"He has had a back or neck injury, Lexi. We don't know how severe it is, but his spinal cord has been traumatized. He is paralyzed right now and on a respirator, but we don't know if the paralysis is permanent or temporary."

"Paralyzed?" The word fell woodenly from Lexi's lips. "You mean he can't walk?"

"Not right now. The doctors have given him a drug that should clear the inflammation around the spinal cord and reduce the swelling. Until the drug takes effect, he must remain immobile," Mrs. Winston explained.

Lexi wanted to cry out, but instead asked quietly, "Do you think it will help him?"

"I don't know, dear. The doctors are doing all they can for him. If his spinal cord is only traumatized but not severed, the outlook for his recovery is optimistic." Mrs. Winston rubbed Lexi's back in an effort to massage away the tension. "There's no way to tell at this point exactly what the outcome will be."

Lexi nodded silently, tears welling up in her eyes.

"I know your faith is strong, Lexi," Mrs. Winston said, "and you will need to rely on that now. Your prayers for us and for Todd are a big factor in this."

"But it doesn't seem like enough. I should be doing more."

"There isn't any more you can do. We have excellent doctors here. Todd is getting the very best medical care he can get. Cedar River is one of the few cities with a spine trauma unit. The only other thing we *can* do is to tap into the greatest Power Source in the universe; to call on our loving Heavenly Father to see us through this, and, most of all, to heal Todd. It's not a small thing I'm asking you to do, Lexi, it's a big one."

"I guess you're right, Mrs. Winston. I know what

God did for me when I was trying to work through my grandfather's death and my grandmother's diagnosis of Alzheimer's disease," Lexi admitted. "He got me through those times." She sighed and lifted her eyes upward. "But this time, it sounds like we're going to have to ask for an even bigger miracle."

"I believe so. But who better to ask? God is the one who can make miracles happen."

So it had come to this. Asking God for a miracle. Praying that Todd would not be permanently paralyzed. Lexi had asked for some big things in her young life, but surely no one would argue that this was the biggest.

Egg mumbled something and stretched as he rolled to an upright position. He ran his fingers through his hair until it stood up in spikes. "I didn't mean to fall asleep. Binky, wake up!"

Egg's sister groaned. "What? What time is it, anyway?"

"Almost one o'clock in the morning," Jennifer announced sleepily, staring at her watch.

"How's Todd?" everyone asked at once.

"We still don't have a full diagnosis," Mrs. Winston explained. "I was just telling Lexi that it's time all of you head for home. There's nothing more any of you can do here. I'm sure your parents are wondering why you aren't home yet."

"We called them," Binky assured Mrs. Winston. "They said we could stay as long as you wanted us to."

"That's very thoughtful of them, and of you, but it's getting very late."

Footsteps in the hallway drew everyone's attention to the door. Lexi's parents, Jim and Marilyn Leighton, entered the room. Without a word, Mrs. Leighton went to Mrs. Winston and put her arms around her.

Dr. Leighton, a veterinarian, and perhaps more comfortable than most in a hospital, asked his daughter, "Are you okay?"

Lexi knew her father's words held more meaning than the simple question they implied. "As okay as I can be, under the circumstances."

He smiled and hugged his only daughter. "How about the rest of you?" he said, turning to Egg, Binky and Jennifer. They shrugged, looking bewildered.

Just then Mr. Winston and Mike returned. "Has there been any word?" Mike asked.

Mrs. Winston shook her head. "Nothing more."

"We came to take these young people home," Dr. Leighton explained. "It's getting late."

"They weren't about to leave us," Mrs. Winston said with a faint smile. "We do appreciate their concern, but until we know more, it might be best for everyone to get their rest."

"Get your things together," Mrs. Leighton said. "We'll take everyone home."

Tearfully, the foursome said goodbye to the Winstons. It didn't seem right to be leaving without seeing Todd. To Lexi, the idea of Todd on a respirator—to keep him breathing—left a sick, empty feeling in the pit of her stomach.

"Pile in, everyone," Dr. Leighton said, opening the back door for Jennifer and Binky. "How did you get here anyway?"

"Minda Hannaford," Lexi said. "But she had to leave awhile ago."

"This is absolutely the worst thing that has ever happened to us!" Binky wailed.

"I can't believe it, either," Egg moaned. "I know the coach is always warning us of accidents like this, but no one ever believed it could actually *happen*."

Tears ran down Binky's cheeks. "He looked so quiet out there on the grass. I knew immediately that something was wrong."

"It took forever for the paramedics to get to him," Jennifer added.

"But it wasn't that long," Egg corrected. "The ambulance is always on hand, and Coach Drummond signaled for it right away."

"Well, it *seemed* like forever," Jennifer insisted.

On the ride home, no one could speak of anything but the accident. Everyone had questions about Todd's condition and Lexi was hesitant to tell them what Mrs. Winston had told her.

After the others had been dropped off, they approached the Leighton home, and Lexi wondered about the bright lights in the living room window.

"Who's up?" Lexi asked.

"I hope Benjamin is asleep by now," Mrs. Leighton said. "But we asked Peggy Madison to stay with him."

Of course, Ben would be in bed. Lexi had almost forgotten about her little brother. Ben, who had Down's syndrome, could not be left alone, but usually Lexi was the one who stayed with him when her parents were out.

They were halfway up the sidewalk when the front door flew open and Peggy, their neighbor and Lexi's friend, came rushing out. Without a word, the girls clung to each other.

Peggy had also been at the hospital briefly and had shared Lexi's pain and grief. The two had been through a great deal together in the past year. Peggy was still recovering from her former boyfriend's suicide. He was the father of the baby Peggy had given up for adoption during the past school year.

"I'd better be going." Peggy squeezed Lexi's hand and turned to Dr. and Mrs. Leighton. "Ben didn't even wake up."

"Let me pay you," Dr. Leighton said, reaching for his wallet.

"I wouldn't dream of taking money for watching Ben," Peggy assured him. "Not after all your family has done for me. Thank you for asking me."

"Thank you for being so kind," Mrs. Leighton said.

"Let me walk you home at least," Mr. Leighton insisted. "It's really too late to be walking even a short distance."

Lexi said good night, mounted the stairs to her room, and closed the door. Before preparing for bed, she dropped to her knees in prayer.

Chapter Two

"Time to get up, Lexi." Mrs. Leighton poked her head through Lexi's bedroom door. "If you don't hurry, you're going to be late."

Lexi slid her feet into the slippers beside her bed. "I don't want to go to school this morning. I'd rather go to the hospital. Maybe they'll have some news about Todd."

Yesterday had been spent waiting for news—any news—about the extent of Todd's injuries and the doctors' prognosis. Even the hour in church was spent praying for Todd and his healing.

"I've already called the hospital, Lexi," her mother said. "I talked to Todd's mother, and she said they will remove the respirator today, so he can breathe on his own. That's good news. She promised to call as soon as she heard anything more."

A brief sense of relief flooded through Lexi. "I'd feel better if I could be there with him."

"I know, dear, but I think you should go to school. Todd isn't going to be better overnight. This is going to take time. You have to go on with your life."

Go on with my life? Lexi thought, then she blurted, "What about his life?"

Mrs. Leighton put her arm around her daughter. "It's in God's hands, Lexi. We just have to keep on praying."

Lexi turned grimly to face her mirror. "Mom! I look like a ghost!"

"You are pale," her mother agreed. "You'd better get to bed extra early tonight."

Lexi moaned as her mother left the room. She pulled through her hair with a brush. For the first time in a long time, she didn't care how she looked or what she wore to school. Her outward appearance might as well match how she felt. She pulled on a pair of jeans and chose a plain sweatshirt from her drawer. After gathering her books into a bag she descended the stairs to the kitchen.

"I know you don't have time to sit down, Lexi, but I've fixed you a piece of toast with peanut butter and jelly."

"Oh, Mom," Lexi sighed.

"You probably don't feel like eating, but it will get you through the morning."

Lexi took the toast and a napkin and started out the door.

Peggy met her at the middle of the block. "Have you heard anything?" she blurted, without even saying hello.

Before Lexi could answer, a yell caught their attention. Jennifer, Egg and Binky were hiking rapidly up the side street. "Wait up!" Egg waved his hand in the air. "Wait for us."

"What a pitiful group we are," Peggy observed as they all met at the corner and exchanged questions and concerns about Todd.

"What do you mean by that?" Jennifer asked.

Peggy shrugged. "We took Todd for granted. He was the one who always picked us up for school. Now we're barely going to make it in time for the first bell."

As they hurried on their way, everyone spoke of their relief that Todd would be taken off the respirator today. No one had the courage to express their true fears.

The hall at the school's main entrance became quiet when Lexi and the others entered. Lexi felt like everyone was staring at her.

"Lexi, have you heard anything?" someone asked.

"Nothing yet."

It had been thirty-six hours since Todd entered the hospital. Everyone was waiting on pins and needles for news of his fate, but the doctors were still closemouthed. Until the swelling went down, they were unwilling to predict anything about their patient's condition.

After their first class, Minda, Tressa, and Gina—members of the High-Fives—met Lexi at her locker. Normally the girls in this exclusive club were a cocky bunch, but this morning even they were subdued.

"Lexi . . ." Minda began.

"All we know is that Todd will be taken off the respirator today," Lexi blurted. "Mom called the hospital this morning, and Mrs. Winston didn't have any more news."

"I just wanted you to know that we are all thinking of you and Todd, Lexi."

Tressa Williams touched Lexi's shoulder. "I know I haven't always been much of a friend to you, Lexi, but I'm real sorry about what happened to Todd. I'm sorry for you, too."

"Thanks, Tressa. I appreciate that." Lexi blinked away the tears that threatened to spill over. "It's pretty hard not knowing any more than we do."

"Todd'll be all right," Gina interrupted. "We know he will. He's tough."

"I hope so," Lexi said. "But this is awfully serious."

"We're sure he'll be okay," Minda said. "I know lots of the kids have been praying for Todd."

Lexi looked startled. "They have?"

Gina looked embarrassed. "I know we don't seem like the praying type, Lexi, but when things get really bad and there's nowhere else to turn, you realize maybe that's the only answer." She shrugged. "Anyway, we don't know what else to do."

"What was that all about?" Jennifer asked as soon as Minda and her friends had gone.

"They said they were *praying* for Todd."

Jennifer whistled through her teeth. "Stranger things have happened, but not many."

"I think it's great that they're praying—and admitting it," Lexi said as she stuffed her books into her locker. "This accident has made everybody think about life in a new way."

"That's for sure." Jennifer leaned against the wall and gazed thoughtfully down the hall. "I used to think that nothing could happen to any of us. That we were . . . what's the word? . . . invincible. I thought bad things only happened to older people. But that's not necessarily so, is it?"

"Lots of bad things happen to young people, Jennifer. Besides Todd's injury, there was Chad's suicide. And remember the time my brother Ben was hit by Jerry Randall's car?"

Jennifer nodded. "Growing up isn't as much fun as I thought it would be," she admitted. "I feel so sorry for Mr. and Mrs. Winston too."

"I know," Lexi agreed. "When I look at Todd's mother, I feel like crying. She's so scared, yet she's trying to be strong for the rest of us."

"We'll have to be the ones strong for her." Jennifer had a determined look. "We're going to have to make the best of this no matter what happens."

Make the best of it, no matter what, Lexi thought. Could they do that? Could they make the best of an injury that might leave Todd paralyzed?

Lexi's mind flew back to the preceding weeks when Chad Allan, their classmate and friend, had committed suicide. When things had gone sour for Chad, he certainly hadn't made the best of it. He'd lost his girlfriend and his self-respect. Ultimately he'd decided to take his own life.

Could Todd make the best of a bad situation?

Lexi sank into her desk chair as the bell rang for their next class. Mrs. Waverly came bustling into the room. Her pale blonde hair was piled high atop her head in its usual manner. A pencil stuck out from the back at an odd angle.

"Attention, class," she began. "I think it would be good if we took a few minutes to talk about the accident on the football field on Saturday."

Mrs. Waverly paused a moment as everyone stopped talking and turned toward the front of the room. The silence was uncomfortable for Lexi.

"I know many of you still have questions about Todd Winston's injuries. I just spoke to his mother at the hospital. There has been no further word on the extent of the damage done to his spine. There is still some swelling, so the diagnosis cannot be completed. The doctors are not saying one way or the other about his chances of full recovery. But Todd's parents haven't given up hope, and neither should we."

"Is he paralyzed?" someone asked.

"He has what is called *impaired function*. He can move his hands but doesn't have complete use of them. His mother says he can make a fist but not open his hand again," Mrs. Waverly explained.

Lexi flexed her fingers, trying to imagine what it would be like. She couldn't. *Todd has to get well! He just has to.*

Several other questions were raised and Lexi tried not to think about them, until Tim Anders spoke up from the back of the room: "He will walk again, won't he?"

"We certainly hope so, Tim. We simply don't know at this point. And although this is a very terrifying time for all of us, we ask that you try to remain calm, and address concerns or worries you may have to the school counselors. They are available all day for anyone who would like to talk to them. You don't need an appointment. If you'd like to talk to a counselor, tell a teacher in any of your classes, and he or she will issue you a pass. Is that clear?"

"You mean we can skip class to talk to a counselor?" a surprised student asked.

Mrs. Waverly smiled faintly. "Yes. Otherwise, the

best we can do is proceed as usual. Keeping our minds busy will help keep anxieties under control.

"Several of you have asked when Todd can have visitors. He is still in intensive care, but as soon as he can have company Mrs. Winston will call us at the school. Meanwhile, I've printed the address of the hospital on the board. Anyone who would like to write to Todd or his parents is welcome to do so.

"Now then," Mrs. Waverly said, reaching for the pencil tucked in her hair, "class will proceed as usual."

Though Lexi tried to pay attention, it was difficult to concentrate. By the time she'd met her friends in the cafeteria at lunchtime, she wasn't sure if she'd grasped anything in her classes.

Matt Windsor and Anna Marie Arnold joined Lexi's usual group. "Hi, Lexi. How's it going?" Matt gave Lexi a sympathetic look.

"Not too great."

"We were just talking about the accident," Anna Marie interjected. "We still can't believe it happened."

"It was so quick," Egg said, with a shake of his head. "Todd was fine one second and the next—*Bang*—he was on the ground."

"Don't they really know anything?" Anna Marie asked, frustration in her voice. "How long will it be?"

"I looked up some stuff in the library," Binky announced. "The book I found said that spinal cord injuries take a long time to heal. That means Todd could be laid up for ages."

Anna Marie nodded. "I knew a guy who was in a motorcycle accident once and he . . ."

Matt laid his hand on Anna Marie's arm. "Maybe we'd better not discuss it. Lexi looks like she's about to faint."

Lexi couldn't take any more of this conversation. She didn't want to hear another word about Todd's injuries. She felt as though she were crumbling inside.

Chapter Three

The distinctive hospital odor struck Lexi full force and made her cringe. She took a deep breath and for a few seconds felt dizzy, almost nauseous. She clutched nervously at the handful of string threaded through her fingers. A cluster of bright mylar balloons bobbed cheerily overhead. The shimmery yellow, blue and silver seemed out of place in the sterile, antiseptic-smelling hallway.

"May I help you?" A volunteer in a pale blue jacket greeted her.

"Oh, yes. Uh—may I take these balloons into intensive care?" Lexi wondered, the sound of her own voice sounding surprisingly weak and trembly in her ears.

"Of course," the woman said, smiling. "They'll cheer the place up a bit."

Lexi walked to the elevators and pressed the button. The *up* arrow flashed red and in a moment the doors slid open. She reeled in the balloons so as not to catch them in the doors as she stepped in. A young orderly stood inside with an elderly man in a wheelchair. When he smiled at Lexi she relaxed.

"How are you today?" he asked, his eyes fixed on

the bobbing balloons. "Those are cheery. Must be for someone special."

"Yes," Lexi murmured, feeling a slight blush rise in her cheeks. She'd had no idea what to bring Todd and even less of an idea what to expect when she saw him.

When the elevator halted at the intensive care floor, Lexi's stomach gave a lurch. The strong anti-septic odor wafted in as the doors opened. The hall was unusually long and bright, littered with wheel-chairs and chart carts. Lexi clutched the balloons as though they were a lifeline and started down the hallway.

Most of the patients' rooms were open, and al-though Lexi tried not to stare, she found her eyes drawn toward the people in the rooms. A young boy lay in traction, his leg slung high in the air in an intimidating brace of loops and pulleys.

In another room, an elderly man was strapped in a wheelchair. He tapped his fingers on the arm of the chair while gazing listlessly at the television hung on the wall. Lexi's stomach turned at the sight of anyone suffering; the thought of Todd injured was almost more than she could bear.

"Hello, Lexi," a friendly voice called to her.

It was Todd's mother. She looked young and frag-ile in a casual outfit of cotton slacks and blouse. Lexi was accustomed to seeing Mrs. Winston in business suits and heels.

"I'm so glad you came." Mrs. Winston walked to-ward Lexi, her arms open to embrace her. Lexi was surprised at how thin and delicate Mrs. Winston felt against her. She always thought of her as stronger—

an assertive, confident woman. Todd's injuries had affected her. She seemed vulnerable now, her strength drained. She would need to draw encouragement from others. Lexi would try to be of help to her in any way she could.

"The nurses are with Todd now," Mrs. Winston explained. "They sent me out for a few minutes. We can wait can't we?"

"Of course." Lexi smiled and relaxed. "We'll wait as long as we have to."

"Why don't we go to the family sitting room on this floor," Mrs. Winston suggested. "It's close by. You can harness those balloons and have a soda. How does that sound?"

Lexi nodded, realizing that her mouth was dry. When they reached the room, Mrs. Winston pulled some quarters out of her pocket. "What would you like, Lexi? Juice? Soda? Mineral water?"

"Mineral water sounds good." Lexi glanced around the room. It was decorated similarly to the room where they'd waited downstairs when Todd was first admitted to the hospital.

"Todd's father and I have spent many hours in this room," Mrs. Winston commented. "It's okay for a waiting room, but you don't get a very good night's sleep here."

"Where's Mr. Winston today?" Lexi asked, trying to imagine what it would be like to sleep in such a room.

"He had to go to work for a while. Mondays are pretty busy and he thought he should check up on some of the more urgent matters." She glanced at her watch. "He should be back shortly. Mike offered to help out, but he has his own work too."

"How *is* Todd doing, Mrs. Winston? I mean, *really.*" Lexi searched Mrs. Winston's eyes intently.

"As hard as it is to believe, we don't know much more than we did two days ago, Lexi. The doctors are pretty certain his spinal cord is intact, but until the swelling and inflammation decrease they can't say for sure."

Lexi felt cold and clammy. She didn't like the uncertainty of this. Things like this happened to *other* people—not to her friends!

Mrs. Winston laid her hand on Lexi's arm. "Before we go into Todd's room, I just want to warn you: There's lots of sophisticated equipment—monitors and such. So don't be alarmed. They're taking very good care of Todd at this hospital."

Lexi nodded, hoping she could manage seeing Todd attached to anything so alarming.

"His neck is in traction, and he's in a big bed that rotates from side to side to keep his circulation moving," Mrs. Winston went on. "It tips at a 45-degree angle—first to the right, then to the left. There are hoses around his legs to aid circulation. Many of these things are precautionary."

Lexi was beginning to feel sick to her stomach.

Mrs. Winston could see the worry on her face. "I'm sorry, dear, but I thought it best to at least warn you. I didn't know if you had any idea what to expect. Don't let Todd frighten you either, Lexi."

"Todd? Frighten me?" Lexi was startled by her statement.

"Todd is having some trouble, emotionally," Mrs. Winston said bluntly. "He's been a very strong, active boy, as you know. To suddenly be immobilized in a hospital bed is terrifying for him. He's afraid he may be limited in some way as a result of his injuries."

"You mean, he's worried about being p—paralyzed?" Lexi hated the sound of the awful word.

"He struggles with the possibility, Lexi." Mrs. Winston forced a smile. "But he's still Todd. He'll come around. I'm sure just seeing you will be a tremendous encouragement to him."

"Oh, Mrs. Winston, I hope so. It must be awful for him, for your whole family."

"He's handling this as well as can be expected under the circumstances. But sometimes he's angry with the whole thing, and becomes easily frustrated."

"Of course!" Lexi understood very well. Her grandmother's Alzheimer's disease had taught her how a person's moods could change from rational to confused, because of the effects of illness or injury.

"I think the nurses should be gone by now," Mrs. Winston said, looking at the clock. "Shall we go see Todd?"

Lexi swallowed the lump in her throat and nodded. When they reached Todd's room, Lexi could see from the hallway the bed his mother had described. She was glad she'd had some warning about the array of medical equipment surrounding it.

The room was a bright yellow. Huge posters of hot air balloons and mountain scenes graced the wall facing Todd's bed. As Lexi passed the curtain that had hid Todd's face from her view, she felt his eyes upon her. She took a deep breath and managed to smile. "Hello, Todd."

"Hi," came the faint monosyllabic response.

"I brought you some balloons." Lexi looked for a place to put them. "I tied washers to the strings so they wouldn't float away."

"Why don't you put them in the corner?" Mrs. Winston pointed.

"They're beautiful, Lexi, aren't they, Todd?"

"Beautiful." His face was pale, his eyes were smudged, dark circles. His golden blond hair was tousled and stuck to his forehead. The bed moved slowly from side to side, its patient swathed in tubes and equipment. A droning hum filled the room. Lexi was strangely at a loss for words.

Todd looked stiff and uncomfortable, and stared straight ahead.

Lexi thought her heart would break, but she knew she had to make conversation. No one else was saying anything.

"Ben said to say hi, Todd. He was very upset when I told him he couldn't come to see you."

"Say hi to him for me," Todd said softly. "It's good to see you, Lexi."

Lexi felt a rush of happiness fill her in spite of the trying circumstances. "My mom and dad are going to visit you soon, but they thought I should come first." She gave a little laugh. "I agreed with them. Dad said you might be interested to know that one of his patients is a dog that's really seventy-five percent wolf. He got his paw caught in a trap. He's mean-looking. Not my idea of a pet." Lexi felt like she was rambling on to herself.

Todd smiled faintly but didn't say any more. He looked smaller than usual. It was so hard to see him immobile when he'd always been so alive and active.

"Do you like the posters?" Lexi gestured toward them. "If you'd like, I could bring some others down just for a change of scenery."

"It doesn't matter." Todd's voice was weak and vacant. Lexi longed to pull him back to her world, away from the sad place he seemed to have gone.

"You'll have to hurry and get well, Todd," Lexi tried to sound positive. "There are so many pictures we'd planned to take for the school paper. I'm not nearly the photographer you are. I'll do my best, but when you come back—"

Todd cut her off, "*If* I come back . . ."

His words shot through Lexi like a bullet. She cast an anguished glance at Mrs. Winston, but her head was averted.

"I think Todd is getting tired." Mrs. Winston broke the icy silence.

No expression registered on Todd's face, and Lexi longed to reach out and touch his hand. Would her touch hurt him? She was afraid to try.

When they rose to leave, Lexi leaned over the side of the bed and brushed her lips gently across Todd's forehead. "I'll be back," she said. "And I'll be praying for you."

Todd whispered, "Goodbye."

Lexi moved quickly into the hallway, relieved that the visit was over.

"Well, what do you think?" Mrs. Winston asked, a worried expression on her face.

"I don't know what to think. I guess I thought Todd would talk more," Lexi said bluntly.

"Give him some time, Lexi. He's a very sick boy

right now, but we have to hope that he'll get better."

"He seems so lifeless and sad."

"Remember, he can't move. That's all the more reason we have to be here for him, Lexi. I appreciate your coming. You're a good friend."

"If there's anything at all that I can do, will you let me know?" Lexi pleaded.

"Just come to see him, Lexi, and pray for him."

Lexi left Mrs. Winston standing in the hallway as she entered the elevator. "Help us all," Lexi prayed quietly. "Father, help us all out of this terrible mess."

Chapter Four

Lexi felt sad and dejected as she walked toward home. She knew she must look terrible, too. She'd stopped in the park to have a good cry. It wasn't until she mounted the steps of the porch that she noticed Peggy and Jennifer on the lawn chairs.

They looked like mournful statues. Peggy rarely smiled, and this incident with Todd meant one more problem for her to face.

"How is he?" Jennifer demanded in her usual abrupt tone.

"Not so good. I could barely get him to talk. He lies there like he's entombed in that huge moving bed."

Jennifer put her hands over her eyes and shuddered. "I don't want to hear any more."

"Well, he's still alive," Peggy blurted angrily. "He may not be in the best shape, but he's alive . . ."

Both girls knew Peggy was thinking of Chad again, dead at the age of seventeen, by his own hand. Even though Peggy had come a long way toward recovery, her moods and emotions were still unpredictable.

Before anyone could respond, Mrs. Leighton

stepped onto the porch. She made a quick perusal of the girls' faces. "I see you're back, Lexi. How did your visit go?"

"Can we talk about it later, Mom?"

"Of course, dear. I've just had a most interesting telephone call."

"I'm flunking physics and they're calling everyone in town to let them know," Jennifer said matter-of-factly.

Mrs. Leighton chuckled. "Traumatic as a physics grade can be, I don't think the teachers have resorted to that. Guess again."

"Why don't you just tell us, Mom? We're not in the mood for guessing games," Lexi said, trying to keep the edge from her voice.

"I've just had a call from the church. There's good news. They've hired a youth pastor."

"What does a youth pastor do?" Jennifer wondered aloud.

"He ministers to the youth in the church. We've never had one before. I guess we'll have to see what he has planned for you young people."

"Somebody just for *us*?" Lexi looked interested.

"That's right. He's already talking about revamping the youth group."

"Revamping?" Peggy asked. "How about starting from scratch."

Lexi hadn't been very impressed with the group either. She missed the youth group back in Grover's Point where her family had lived before moving to Cedar River. The members there had become close personal friends.

"I think he's come at an absolutely perfect time,"

Mrs. Leighton said, satisfaction in her voice.

"Why's that?" Peggy asked.

"Because you all need something to distract you, keep you busy, occupied. I even took the liberty to suggest to the church secretary that you'd be willing to work with Pastor Lake on the committee to re-vamp the youth group."

All three girls groaned in unison. Mrs. Leighton ignored their sighs. "I don't want to see you sitting on my porch gloomy and bored. You need to get out and do something to keep your minds off your prob-lems."

Lexi agreed. "In a way, you're right, Mom. We've all been so concerned with things happening around here, we've forgetten what we can do that's produc-tive. Working on this project is something we can do for Todd. The church is important to him. When he gets out of the hospital, it would be nice to have some-thing organized."

"How about a party, too," Peggy suggested, her eyes lighting with interest for the first time.

"Yeah! That's a great idea," Jennifer agreed. "Todd's going to need *lots* of activity to cheer him up."

"That's what I hoped to hear," Mrs. Leighton said, and disappeared into the house. When she returned, she had note pads and pencils for the girls. "Why don't you jot your ideas down on paper. There's a meeting at the church tonight. If you go prepared with good ideas, they'll have to listen to you."

"The meeting's tonight?"

"At 7:30." Mrs. Leighton put her hands on her hips. "It's probably none of my business, but I think it would be nice to invite Binky and Egg too. I'd like to see them involved."

The girls nodded enthusiastically. Egg and Binky's presence would certainly help right now.

Jennifer started to write down her ideas. "I'd like us to go on a hay ride," she said. "My cousin's youth group has gone on one and she says it's tons of fun. All you need is a hay wagon, some hay, and a couple of work horses. After a drive in the country, you stop and build a bonfire, roast marshmallows, and sing camp songs."

"Sounds like a pretty simple outing," Peggy said. "But what if we can't find anyone with horses or a hay wagon?"

"I don't think that will be too difficult," Jennifer insisted. "If nothing else, we can still roast marshmallows."

"How about volleyball?" Peggy suggested. "Everyone likes to play volleyball."

"Write it down," Lexi said, relieved that they had something to distract them from thinking about Todd. "One of my favorite things is video discussions."

"Video discussions?" Jennifer looked blank.

"Yes. You watch a movie or documentary together—something interesting and controversial at the same time—and then you have a group discussion about it. It gets people to talk, and you learn more about each other that way."

"That sounds just like you, Lexi—intellectual," Peggy said.

Lexi laughed. "I don't know how intellectual it is, but it's great for starting conversations."

"A taffy pull!" Jennifer exclaimed. "We haven't done that since grade school."

"How does a scavenger hunt sound?" Lexi asked. "With a really difficult list, we could make an evening of it."

Peggy nodded. "We'd have to think of some great prizes for the winning team."

"How about a lock-in?" Jennifer suggested. "We could all spend the night at the church and have Bible studies and play games."

Each tried to top the others with new ideas, their enthusiasm increasing as the list grew. Twenty minutes later Mrs. Leighton emerged with a large pizza. "I thought you'd need some nourishment after expending all your energy on your project."

"We called Binky and Egg, Mom. They're going to meet us at the church!" Lexi enthused.

"Good for you, girls. I'm glad you're all excited about the prospect of something happening at the church for a change."

Lexi marveled at her mother's knack for thinking up ways to encourage her and her friends. The new-youth-group planning project was heaven-sent.

Jennifer, Peggy, and Lexi met Egg and Binky at the entrance to the church, and walked together to the fellowship hall. A young man dressed in jeans and a plaid sportshirt met them at the door.

"Hello, and welcome!" he greeted them genuinely. His dynamic smile was contagious. Lexi knew instinctively he was going to be just what they needed. "My name is Carl Lake and I'm your new youth pastor. I'm glad you could all come out tonight."

The young pastor had short, dark hair, was of

medium height, and had an athletic build. He looked to be in his late twenties, and was brimming with energy and enthusiasm. Lexi liked him immediately.

"I'm happy to meet you, Pastor Lake. I'm Lexi Leighton, and these are my friends: Jennifer Golden, Peggy Madison, Binky McNaughton, and Egg McNaughton."

Carl Lake shook hands with each of them. When he shook Egg's hand he smiled and said, "Egg, huh? Great nickname. They called me Pancake when I was in high school."

"Pancake?"

He smiled, looking a little embarrassed. "Someone dared me to down the leftover pancake batter we'd made at a youth supper."

"You mean you drank it?" Egg was incredulous.

"I'm afraid so," Pastor Lake admitted. "I've never eaten another pancake since. Even the smell of maple syrup makes my stomach churn."

Everyone laughed.

"You don't mind if Binky and I come to this meeting do you?" Egg suddenly felt out of place.

"Mind? Why's that?"

"Because we aren't members of this church," Egg explained.

"Of course not. If only members of the church came here, we wouldn't get any *new* members." Pastor Lake put his arm around Egg's shoulders. "I'm delighted to have all of you join us. There are several people here already. You probably know most of them, but I'm just getting acquainted."

Lexi recognized several young people from the church and a few new ones from school. In no time,

Pastor Lake had everyone seated around a large table, discussing the things they'd like to do in the coming year. Lexi and her friends were glad they had written down some ideas ahead of time.

At the end of the discussion, Carl stood to speak. "I want you to know how happy I am that you've so readily accepted me here. This is my first day on the job and already I feel like I belong here. Thank you. I want to say also that one of the most important things we as Christians can do is to let others see how we love one another, and thereby encourage them to become part of the family of God.

"Fun and fellowship are important too. So please feel free to invite anyone you know to join us. We don't want anyone to feel he or she is not eligible to be a part of our group. There are no membership rules. God wants everyone to come into His house and fellowship with His children."

The young pastor's expression became somber. "Our Father is deeply concerned too about those in our midst who may be suffering a loss or some sort of illness or injury. I am told that a friend of yours, Todd Winston, is in the hospital. Let's keep him in our thoughts and prayers tonight, and throughout the weeks to come.

"Now, before I say any more, I think it's time for some food."

Everyone burst into animated conversation and headed for the kitchen. It was an hour later before Lexi and her friends started for home.

"I really like the new pastor, Lexi!" Egg said as soon as they were outside. "He's a super guy. Your youth group sounds like it should be a lot of fun."

"You mean *our* youth group, Egg," Lexi corrected.

"Yeah, I guess you're right. I'd like to come to all the meetings I can. How about you, Binky?"

"Without a doubt. I think we've been missing out on something."

Lexi knew Binky had been thinking a lot about God lately—especially since Chad's untimely death.

"The youth group is a good place to meet new people, and to learn some things that will help us in our daily lives," Lexi said.

"You know, if *I'm* interested, there must be other kids who would like to know about a group like this," Egg reasoned.

Lexi gave a knowing look.

"What're you thinking?" Jennifer asked bluntly.

"I think God's trying to tell me something," Lexi said softly.

"He is?" Binky looked up into the star-studded sky. "I didn't hear anything."

"It's all this talk about bringing new people into the youth group," Lexi explained. "I have a hunch God wants Minda Hannaford in this group."

"Minda!" Peggy and Jennifer chimed together. "Why her? She'll wreck everything."

"No she won't. She's changed," Lexi admitted. "After Chad died she was concerned about all of us, especially Peggy. And when Todd got hurt, she tried her best to help, by taking me to the hospital and showing she cared about Todd's condition. Actually, I should have invited her to the group a long time ago, but it wasn't very active, so my conscience didn't bother me too much. But tonight, after Pastor Lake gave his enthusiastic speech about the church being open to everyone, I knew I should extend an invitation to Minda and the other High-Fives to join us."

Binky was still looking up at the sky. "God told you that?"

Lexi laughed. "God does tell me things sometimes, Binky. It's like a deep impression in my mind. This time, He's speaking loud and clear. He wants our church to have a strong, active youth group. And we're responsible for making that happen."

"Maybe I don't want to know God any better," Binky admitted. "Sounds like He makes a lot of extra work for a person."

"It won't be a lot of work, Binky. I think we all need a supportive group of friends to help us keep our spirits up, and someone like Pastor Lake to help us know what God has planned for our lives." Lexi sounded convincing.

"There have been days when I wondered if I could go on with my life," Peggy said honestly. "But tonight I forgot about my troubles for a while." She kicked a small stone ahead of her. "How can I be depressed about my life when Todd is lying in a hospital bed wondering if he'll ever walk again?"

Binky groaned. "Who ever said the teenage years are the best years of your life?"

"Probably grandmother," Egg reminded her. "She's too old to remember what it was like."

Lexi's determination was renewed. She and her friends had truly been through some tough times. But life was worth living. She wanted to be an example of one who chose life and lived it to its fullest.

If a newly organized youth group could help anyone in any way at all, she would work as hard as she could to make it happen. Perhaps Pastor Lake was an answer to her prayers.

Chapter Five

Lexi dumped her school books on her bed and glanced at her watch. It was time to go to the hospital. It had been four long days since the accident. She'd made a promise to herself and to Todd that she would visit him every day. But each day it became more difficult to walk through those hospital doors and down the long sterile corridor to Todd's room.

Though the doctors assured Mr. and Mrs. Winston that Todd was making excellent progress, Lexi couldn't see it. He was still paralyzed. That's what counted.

With a soul-weary sigh, she picked up a sweater and walked to the door.

"Going somewhere, honey?" Mrs. Leighton was working on a small water-color painting in the living room. Ben played with his trucks on the floor.

"To the hospital."

"Of course. I should have known."

"I dread it, Mom," Lexi blurted. "He's so . . . *hurt!*"

"I'm sure you do dread it, but Todd needs you. His mother tells me how important it is that you've been such a faithful friend."

"I'd better be going. See you later, Mom, Ben."

"Say hi to Todd, Lexi," Ben called after her.

Lexi rode her bike to the hospital. After securing it in the rack outside, she slowly made her way through the huge double doors.

"You're becoming a familiar face around here," the nurse on Todd's floor greeted her.

Lexi wrinkled her nose. "I know. I wish I could be a stranger again. Does anyone have any idea when Todd will be getting out of the hospital?"

The nurse shook her head somberly. "Spinal injuries are tricky, Lexi. Todd's had good care and the medication he was given right after the accident seems to have been effective, but you'll needs lots of patience to see him through this."

"I always thought it took patience to wait until Christmas morning to open my presents," Lexi admitted ruefully. "Now I'm beginning to learn what *real* patience is about."

As she neared Todd's room, Lexi could hear the TV droning. She tapped on the door and poked her head inside. Todd was watching TV through the strange, periscope-like glasses he had to wear in order to see the screen on the wall from his position flat on his back. Gently Lexi lifted the odd glasses away from his face. "Hi. What are you watching?"

Todd blinked. "I don't know. Something dumb, I think."

"I'll say it's dumb. You're watching cartoons."

He managed a weak grin. "No wonder I'm spaced out. Cartoons are all I'm up to lately anyway."

"I don't believe that for a minute," Lexi said cheerfully as she set the glasses on a nearby table. Some of the hoses and monitoring equipment were gone now. The room was beginning to look more inviting. "According to your mom, you've got some good news."

His eyes darted around the ceiling. "What good news could come from here?"

Lexi thought he would have been more pleased. "Your mother said you're moving your fingers!"

"Big deal. Once I close them, I can't get them open again. What good is that?"

"It's a start."

"So what if I can flail my arms around? That doesn't mean I can swing a bat or serve a tennis ball."

"Not yet, but you will. Your mom also told me you had some feeling in your legs when the doctor examined you. If that's not a good sign, I don't know what is!"

"Face it, Lexi. Look at me. I'm hung up in this hospital bed like a puppet on a string. When do you think I'll ever play tennis again?"

"Maybe next summer. Maybe the summer after that. You'll play again. I know you will."

"You're not rooted in reality, Lexi." Todd's voice was tainted with bitterness. Lexi hated to see him so depressed and dejected. It took all her willpower not to speak to him in the same tone. Instead, she tried to be light and cheerful.

"Tsk, tsk, tsk," she clucked. "Are you crabby today? A little depressed? Down in the mouth? You probably need a dose of Dr. Leighton's miracle medicine. Guaranteed to pick you up, to brighten your eyes and put a smile on your face." She reached in her purse and produced a package of homemade fudge. "Here it is. Eat three of these before or after hospital meals."

"Fudge?"

"Just for you. Fresh from the kitchen. I practically had to force Ben to leave it alone, until I'd taken what I wanted for you. He said to say hi, by the way." She unwrapped the package and held a piece to Todd's mouth.

"Hi, Ben." He bit off a corner and let it melt in his mouth, closing his eyes blissfully. "It's great."

"I'm going to take some to the nursing home again, like we used to. Whenever I visit my grandmother, the residents ask where you are and why we haven't been bringing them fudge lately."

"Have you told them about me?"

"Yes. They all wanted me to tell you that they're praying for you."

Todd's eyes glistened with tears. "I hate being so dependent on others, Lexi. I can't even eat a piece of fudge without your help. What good does it do if I can move my arms? Is that so I can push my own wheelchair?"

"It takes time, Todd. The doctors are hopeful that you'll be able to use your arms *and legs* again."

"I just want it to happen *now!*" he spat out the words. "I hate this hospital. I hate this bed. I'm a junior in high school. *That's* where I should be—with my friends, taking pictures for the *Cedar River Review*, and moaning and groaning because I hate physics class."

His face twisted with the grief of loss. "If I ever *do* get out of here, I'll never complain again about physics, or anything else for that matter. Now I know what it is to be in serious trouble." His eyes clouded with tears again. "I'm scared, Lexi. For the first time in my life, I'm really scared. What if I never get out of here?"

It was the first time Todd had allowed Lexi to know how frightened he was. He was not the Todd Winston she knew. He had always been strong, confident and brave. Now he was afraid and depressed. In a matter of seconds, a freak accident had cost him everything.

"Do you want to talk about it?" Lexi asked.

Todd pressed his lips in a grim line. "Why get you depressed? No, I'd rather talk about something else." The wall was up again between Todd's true feelings and his best friend.

"Well, let's see, nothing out of the ordinary happened in school today," she began. "Of course Egg's wardrobe sparked some interest."

A faint smile crossed Todd's lips. "What's he wearing now?"

"He had on one high-top and one loafer for starters. Binky was so embarrassed, she about died. Egg said he was trying to make a fashion statement. Binky says the only statement he made is that he's going crazy."

"What is it with Egg?" Todd wondered aloud. "It isn't like he has no friends and needs to draw attention to himself."

"Who knows how Egg's mind works? The good news is that Egg and Binky both want to become involved in our youth group at church. They came to the planning meeting that the new youth pastor held. Pastor Lake is pretty enthused about all the things we've planned. I think he really likes the kids. Has he been here yet?"

"He came last night and talked to my mother. I guess I was asleep," Todd said, his voice listless again. Lexi wished she could think of something that would lighten Todd's mood.

"The Emerald Tones rehearsed today," she said. "We missed your tenor voice, Todd. Mrs. Waverly said we'd have to work on the pieces again as soon as you're back."

"You better tell her to find another tenor. It might be a long wait between practices."

"Todd, don't say that." Lexi was getting irritated.

He closed his eyes in response.

"Oh, I do have more news!" she remembered. "Jennifer and Matt are dating."

"What's new about that? They've dated on and off before."

"This was a *real* date. He took her out for dinner."

"Yeah, right. To the Hamburger Shack?" Todd asked sarcastically.

"No, to the Station."

"When did he get to be such a big spender?"

"I suppose he saved up from his summer job." Between Todd and Peggy, Lexi wondered if she'd ever be around happy people again.

As if reading her mind, Todd asked, "How's Peggy doing?"

"A little better. She's working out with the girls' basketball team, but since she was bumped from the starting line, her heart isn't really in it."

"She's as good or better than all the starters," Todd said matter-of-factly.

"I think so too, but Peggy isn't convinced of it.

Her lack of confidence since Chad's death really affects her game."

Peggy couldn't get beyond blaming herself for her boyfriend's suicide. Because he'd threatened to harm himself if she refused to date him again, she felt it was her fault, even though Lexi and everyone else were sure it wasn't.

Of course, Peggy's troubles began with her pregnancy a year ago, and her subsequent decision to give her baby up for adoption. Lexi respected Peggy for refusing to give in to Chad's insistence that their relationship continue on an intimate basis. And because Chad wouldn't have it any other way, Peggy couldn't date him at all.

"I've been thinking about Chad Allan a lot lately," Todd went on.

"Have you?" Lexi asked, not wanting to get into the circumstances of his death again, but glad that Todd was initiating a subject of conversation.

"Maybe I'd be better off like Chad," Todd said morbidly.

Lexi was shocked. "Todd! How can you say something like that?"

"Well, look at me. I'm half dead anyway."

"No you're not, Todd Winston! I don't want to hear you talk like this. It isn't fair to me, and it isn't fair to yourself."

"I'm sorry, Lexi. But it's so frustrating not to be able to do anything for myself. I can't even straighten my pillow."

"But you're getting more feeling, more movement in your limbs every day. You've got to think of the positive things that are happening, Todd."

Todd was silent for a moment. "I'd really like to work on a car in my brother's garage. How many days is *that* going to take?"

"No one knows, Todd. Maybe a lot of days, maybe a few."

"That's just it, Lexi. No one knows if or when I'll get back on my feet. No one will tell me anything."

"Your mother says it will take time. You've only been here four days, Todd!"

"Well, it seems more like four years. And my mother's an optimist. I'm a realist. I've thought a lot about it while I've been lying here, Lexi. I've asked myself, 'Is it worth living if I have to live like this?' I've got to face that."

Lexi was horrified into silence.

"I decided I'd be better off dead." Todd read the pain in Lexi's eyes. "Or aren't I supposed to say or even think that? Is that something that should never enter a Christian's mind?"

Lexi considered the question for a while before answering. Then, surprising herself and Todd, she shook her head. "I suppose thinking about being better off dead isn't wrong in itself," she admitted. "Christian people, just like anyone else, can have low points in their lives, troubles that are beyond their own strength. I learned from my experiences with my grandparents that being a Christian doesn't mean you never have any problems. But I do think Christians, through Christ, can handle what comes to them. That is, *if* they have the courage to call upon Him for strength."

It was Todd's turn to be silent. Finally he spoke: "Well, I'm not doing too well handling this one. I've prayed, but I don't see any answers coming. Every day I wake up and think for a second that everything's normal. Then I remember where I am—trapped in this body, stuck in this bed. I get so discouraged I feel like crying."

Lexi moved closer and touched his hand.

"But if I cry, I can't even wipe away the tears. I have to just let them dry on my face, or call for a nurse. Can you imagine how humiliating that is, Lexi? Usually I just lie here, stubbornly holding back the tears, numb with grief and no way to shake it off . . . no way to get rid of the feelings I have."

Lexi didn't have any more words of comfort to offer. It was hard for her to imagine what it would be like to be as immobile as Todd was, with no certainty that it would ever be any different.

"I try to think about my future and I can't even see myself, Lexi. Am I in a wheelchair? On crutches? Am I walking? Am I even around? Sometimes I think I hear a voice in my head saying God isn't listening to me; He can't answer my prayers because I don't have enough faith. The voice is taunting: 'Just give it up. Just end it all.' "

"Do you know whose voice that is?" Lexi asked.

Todd looked at her blankly. "My own, I suppose."

"No, Todd. It's Satan's voice. He's trying to take advantage of your suffering. He's found you at a weak point. Don't you think lots of people at one time or another have felt like you do? Others have thought their whole lives were coming apart and the best thing would be to end it all. When my grandmother first became ill, I was frightened and ashamed. I wondered why God had given me such a burden to carry. I thought it wasn't fair, and I didn't like it. I wanted the hurting to stop.

"Still, in my heart I knew that I loved, feared and respected God. I couldn't harm myself any more than I could harm anyone else. I am God's temple. I also remembered Exodus 20:13."

"Don't just give me the scripture reference, Lexi. Either tell me what it says or don't bring it up." Todd's voice was impatient.

"Thou shalt not kill," Lexi said evenly. "It's one of the Ten Commandments. And it refers to taking one's own life as well as taking the life of another human being."

A flicker of interest lit Todd's eyes. "I guess I never thought about it that way."

"You're brave and strong and capable, and with God's help you're going to make it through this." Lexi squeezed Todd's unresponsive hand.

When Todd was silent for some time, with his eyes closed, Lexi decided she'd said enough and it was time to leave. She whispered goodbye and left the room quietly.

She hurried down the corridor, anxious to avoid the nurses who often spoke to her when she left the hospital. She didn't feel like talking now. She had to think.

Removing her bike from the rack she hurriedly pushed off toward home. But when she arrived, there was no one around.

She found a note in the kitchen. *I've taken Ben to buy shoes. Be back by suppertime. Mom.*

Lexi felt strangely at odds with herself. Normally, arriving home to peace and quiet would have

been inviting. But after her frustrating visit with
Todd, she needed someone to unload on. She felt like
a volcano ready to erupt. Her first impulse was to
dial the Winston home. She let the phone ring several times, but then remembered Todd's mother had
gone back to work part-time.

The four walls seemed to scream at her, so Lexi
went outside and mounted her bike again. She rode
aimlessly for a while, trying to dissipate some of the
energy she felt building inside.

She soon found herself only a block away from
the church. *Maybe there will be someone there I can
talk to,* Lexi thought, as she pedaled toward the brick
structure.

There were no cars in the parking lot, but a bi-
cycle indicated someone might be inside. Lexi parked
her own bike and entered the sanctuary. Light
streamed through the stained-glass windows, and
the peaceful setting made her feel like sitting in one
of the pews rather than searching the offices for
whoever was still at work.

Deep in thought, Lexi turned her anxiety and
confusion into silent prayer, unburdening her soul
before the Lord. Before she had finished, she felt
someone sit down beside her. She looked up into the
face of the youth pastor.

"Pastor Lake."

"I'm sorry if I've disturbed you, Lexi. But I was
just going to leave, and wondered if you wanted to
talk with someone."

"Actually I did. I've just come from visiting Todd
at the hospital."

The pastor nodded. "I've heard quite a bit about

him. I tried to visit him yesterday but he was asleep, so I had a long conversation with his mother."

"Todd told me." Lexi turned to face him. "I'm really quite concerned about Todd, Pastor Lake. These past four days have been the most agonizing days of my life. I've tried to deal with the fact that Todd has been seriously injured and we won't know the results of his injuries for some time. I want to encourage him to believe the best and trust God to get him through this no matter what the outcome, but it's like he doesn't want to hear it from me. He puts me off, says things like he'd like to just end it all. That is so painful for me, Pastor Lake. Todd and I have been best friends."

Lexi felt like bursting into tears, but felt awkward around the young, new pastor. "I never dreamed Todd would ever think that way. I couldn't believe the words came from his mouth. I thought he was a strong Christian."

"When you stop to think, Lexi, it's really not hard to imagine why Todd feels the way he does. He's a young, healthy man who's suddenly found himself flat on his back in a hospital bed with no assurance that he'll ever be able to walk again—to live a normal life. It's enough to depress anyone. Christian or not."

"Well, of course, but . . ."

"The human survival instinct is very strong, but when someone is young and vulnerable and at such a distinct disadvantage, it would be easy to think the best solution is to escape the suffering and end it all."

"I suppose. But it's not rational!"

"Maybe not. But Todd isn't the first Christian who's ever thought of suicide. Even David, a strong figure in the Bible, considered suicide. He was a desperate man when he wrote Psalm 55: 'I'm frightened inside. The terror of death has attacked me. I'm scared and shaken. Terror grips me. I said, I wish I had wings like a dove . . . I would hurry to my place of escape far away from the wind and storm.'

"David thought not only his friends and family had forsaken him, but God had forsaken him too. He was angry with God." Pastor Lake took a Bible from the rack in front of him. "There's more: 'My life is full of troubles. I am nearly dead. You'd think I'm on the way to my grave. I am like a man with no strength. I have been left for dead like a body lying in a grave. You don't remember dead people. They're cut off from your care . . . I'm almost in the dark place of the dead . . . I am trapped and cannot escape. My eyes are weak from crying.' "

He looked up at Lexi. "Now *that's* a depressed man."

"Wow! I never knew that about David. I always thought of him as the strong man who killed Goliath."

"Most people do. But during his time of trouble, as recorded in Psalm 102, he compared himself to a lonely bird sitting on a housetop, or like dried grass whose days are nothing more than a passing shadow. His self-confidence was gone. When David got to this point in his life, he contemplated suicide."

"What made him change his mind?"

"I think he finally quit pitying himself and turned to God."

"So Todd has to turn to God and ask Him to give him a new outlook, to renew his faith, to make the best of a bad situation."

"I think you've got it, Lexi. God may choose to use you or me or someone else in the process, but Todd needs to reach out and accept the help."

"What can we do meanwhile?" Lexi wondered. "We can't just let him lie there and be depressed."

Pastor Lake glanced at his watch. "It's almost suppertime. Why don't I call Todd's parents? They should be home by now. I'd like to tell them what you've told me, if that's okay. It sounds like Todd is sending out a signal for help. He doesn't really want to die. We need to do all we can to give him as many opportunities as possible to receive the help he needs."

Lexi felt a little better after Pastor Lake left to make the phone call. Still, she was frightened for Todd. It was hard to imagine he hadn't learned anything from the nightmare Chad had created for himself and others. The choice Chad had made didn't come with a second chance. Surely Todd would not consider the same destructive path!

Lexi walked out of the church and picked up her bike. She knew she should go straight home, but decided instead to try to catch her father before he left his office. Maybe he had some more answers.

"Lexi! What a surprise." Dr. Leighton greeted her with a smile. "I thought you'd be helping your mother with supper about this time."

"Yeah, Dad. I should be, but I needed to talk to you for a few minutes without interruption."

"Of course. Come on in to the more comfortable chairs."

Lexi followed her father into his casual office lined with posters depicting every animal imaginable. Medical books covered one wall, and a saddle was draped over a sawhorse in the corner. There were pictures of Ben, her mother, and Lexi herself on the desk.

Her father still displayed on his bulletin board some of the artwork Lexi had done when she was in grade school.

"So, what is it, Lexi?" Dr. Leighton asked.

Without any further coaxing, Lexi poured out to her father her almost-one-sided conversation with Todd at the hospital, and her talk with Pastor Lake at the church. Her father listened intently, compassionately, without any attempt to interrupt her.

"Frankly, I think Pastor Lake gave you some good insight, Lexi. Todd certainly isn't the first person in the world to think of suicide and he won't be the last. People have looked for ways out of situations far less serious than the one Todd is in right now."

"That's what I'm beginning to realize."

"Paul and Silas come to my mind. They were locked in jail because some people in Philippi thought they were causing trouble. Then there was the earthquake in the middle of the night that shook the prison until the doors came open. You remember that the jailer in charge woke up and seeing the doors open, was afraid the prisoners he was responsible for had escaped."

Lexi nodded. She remembered Pastor Horace preaching on this story from the Bible. Her dad continued:

"The jailer got his sword and was about to kill himself, when Paul yelled to the man: 'Don't hurt yourself! We are all here!' In effect, Paul was saying,

'Don't commit suicide. You're not in trouble. Your prisoners haven't escaped.' The jailer was so shaken by the experience that he ran inside and immediately asked Paul and Silas what he had to do to be saved."

"That is quite a story, Dad, but I'm not sure exactly how it relates to Todd."

"Well, the jailer nearly wasted his life because he *thought* he was in deep trouble. Then, just in time, he saw that what he needed was help above and beyond himself. Paul and Silas told him: 'Believe in the Lord Jesus and you will be saved—you and all the people in your house.' It's as simple as that, Lexi. Todd has to turn to the One who changes lives, the only One who can help in a desperate situation."

"But Todd's already a Christian. Why doesn't he automatically turn to Christ for help?" Lexi was confused.

"Because Satan's at work too, Lexi. He's using this opportunity, when Todd is weak and vulnerable, to draw him away from God. Todd is right in the middle of the struggle. Todd has to come to the realization that as long as we have God in our lives, no situation is hopeless. It isn't ours to choose when we will die. Committing suicide deprives God of the opportunity to perform a miracle. Suicide ends the hope. With God there is always hope."

Lexi was quiet and somber. She had in her own way tried to tell Todd the same thing, but somehow her dad had made it even clearer. She hoped Todd would understand before it was too late.

Her father stood to put his arm around her. "It's all going to work out, Lexi. I really believe that. I've been praying for Todd and for you a lot lately."

"Thanks, Dad. I'm really glad I have parents who care for me, and who believe in God and in prayer. I really need help knowing just how to respond to Todd's grief and anger, and how to help him deal with it."

"Just be yourself, Lexi. Continue to be his friend, on hand to help, to listen—even when he's angry, sad or depressed. The other thing you can do, of course, is to pray. Pray for strength for his mind and his heart, strength to resist negative thoughts and attitudes. And pray for healing. God can do a miracle."

Lexi was weary. It had been a long day. She thought a miracle was just what they needed.

Chapter Six

Lexi dressed for the first church youth group meeting, wishing Todd could join them. She had taken their friendship for granted. They had done everything together. Now it was a struggle to think of going to the group without him.

Recovering from a spinal cord injury was torturously slow, and every day, with Lexi's help, Todd had to make a conscious decision not to give up his battle to walk again.

In a different sense, the youth group struggled too, with its first, tentative steps toward a reorganized unit that would serve the young people of the community.

"Ready, Lexi?" Jennifer asked, poking her head into Lexi's bedroom.

"Almost. Where's Peggy?"

"She's downstairs talking with your mother."

"Oh, good. My mom has really been a help to her lately."

Jennifer flung herself across Lexi's bed. "Do you know if Minda and her friends are coming to our meeting?"

"I think so. Sometimes I wonder if I did the right

thing inviting them to the group. Maybe they aren't ready for it yet."

"My question is, are we ready for them?" Jennifer remarked.

Lexi slipped on her shoes. "Come on. Let's go."

The church basement was already full when they arrived. Egg and Binky were at the far end of the room, hovering over the snack table.

"Ready to eat already, Egg?" Lexi asked when they got closer.

Egg was studying the array of bars and cookies. "I'm just checking them out in advance so I know which ones to take when the time comes."

"Yeah, right. All of them," Binky quipped. "You're such a pig, Egg."

"Well, you're a piglet, then," Egg retorted.

"Come on, you guys, let's not get going with your usual bickering," Jennifer pleaded.

"Thanks to Egg, I have to do all my homework over," Binky whispered loudly.

"You were the one who left your homework on the front porch right under the water sprinkler."

"And how was I supposed to know you'd pick to-night to water the lawn? And since when is the porch part of the lawn?" Binky was beginning to raise her voice when the youth pastor called for attention.

"Attention, everyone. Why don't we find seats so we can begin."

Lexi was relieved the meeting was going to start on time. Egg and Binky were starting to get on her nerves.

"I'm going to hand out to each of you a typed list of suggestions for the year's activities that some of you came up with at our planning meeting," Pastor Lake began. "There are some great ideas here. It doesn't mean we will do all of them, but it's a start, and we can add to it as we go along."

Minda, Tressa, and Gina peered at the list together and started to giggle. Minda crumpled the paper in her hand. "It does look pretty boring, doesn't it?"

The girls were sitting close to the front, and Pastor Lake spoke up. "Excuse me. Did you say something?"

"This list of activities." Minda held up the crumpled paper. "It's so childish."

Pastor Lake was unruffled. "Really?"

"How can you expect kids to come to anything like this? Taffy pulls and hayrides? Come on! What about parties? Dancing—something fun."

"Yeah," Gina chimed in, bolstered by Minda's boldness. "How can you expect people to come if you're going to do kid's stuff with them?"

"There's no way *we'd* be interested unless you have a dance or some kind of a party," Tressa agreed.

"Are you threatening not to come back?" Jennifer asked in a hopeful voice.

"I didn't say that," Minda retorted.

"Could have fooled me," someone muttered.

"Maybe it would be better if you didn't come to our meetings," Jennifer blurted. "With an attitude like yours, I don't see how you'd fit in anyway."

Just when Lexi wondered why the youth pastor allowed this kind of banter to go on, he laid a restraining hand on Jennifer's shoulder.

Then he turned to Minda and her friends. "I understand what you're saying girls, but I think the kind of activities you're interested in may be more appropriate somewhere else. Here at the church our function and purpose is a little different. First, we want everyone to get to know each other better—we call it fellowship. We also usually have some good food to eat, and try to create an atmosphere where you can feel at home away from home, a place where you can share one another's joys and burdens.

"Eventually, we hope you learn what it means to become part of the family of God. I realize that you might think some of the activities we've suggested sound rather dull, but let's just give them a try. If they don't work, or there's a consensus that we do something different, we're open for more ideas. Let's not judge too hastily what this group is about or what we're attempting to do."

Minda's eyes narrowed as she squirmed in her chair. "I wasn't expecting a five-point sermon," she muttered.

Gina and Tressa looked to Minda for their next move.

"Tell you what, Minda," Pastor Lake said, "tomorrow night we're going to have a Search for Christians party. Frankly, I think it's something you might enjoy. Will you and your friends come and give it a chance?"

"A *Search for Christians* party?" Minda echoed. "I don't even know what that is."

"Me either," Gina admitted.

"I've never heard of it," piped up a regular member.

Pastor Lake smiled. "Then you'll *all* have to come and give it a try."

"Come on, tell us what it means!" Binky chirped.

Pastor Lake gave another conspiring grin. "You'll find out soon enough. Come tomorrow and you'll be pleasantly surprised."

"Can't you give us a hint?" Lexi asked.

"Sure. It's a lot of fun. Wear your oldest clothes and bring something warm—at least a sweater and a hat or scarf."

"Old clothes and hats for a party?" Minda was incredulous.

Lexi was amazed at how unaffected Pastor Lake was by Minda's attitude. He took it in stride, like it was nothing out of the ordinary. "I think there are some refreshments on the table. Feel free to stay as long as you like."

Lexi's friends found a table and rehashed the meeting's discussion over cookies and punch. Egg wasn't so sure the Search for Christians party was going to be as much fun as Pastor Lake implied.

"What's he got up his sleeve, Lexi?" Binky asked. "Sure hope it doesn't mean we have to go door to door asking people what they believe."

"It can't be that," Peggy assured her. "Can it?"

"Don't worry about it," Lexi said. "And let's not let Minda's mood get us down, either."

"Well, she and her friends were certainly rude to Pastor Lake tonight." Binky looked indignant. "I think she's just plain mean."

"She may be thoughtless and a little selfish, but she can be kind, too." Lexi tried to focus on the fact that Minda had been sensitive to Peggy's suffering, and was more than happy to help out when Todd was injured. "We just have to give her a chance."

"You're always trying to give someone a chance, Lexi." Binky's lip protruded in a pout. "You're too good to be true sometimes."

"Oh, come on, Binky, lighten up," Lexi said, laughing. "Why don't you all stop at my house for a while. It's early yet. We can make root beer floats or something."

"Sounds great!" Egg shouted, almost too eagerly.

Binky gave him a disgusted look.

When they arrived at the Leightons', Ben was at the door to greet them. "Hi, guys!" he chirped cheerfully. "How come you're home so early?"

Egg ruffled Ben's hair. "The meeting was cut short because Minda and her gang got a little obnoxious."

"Oh, what does *ob-knocks-us* mean?" Ben asked.

"Rude and disgusting," Jennifer explained.

"Come on, we can't dwell on a few off-handed remarks," Lexi pleaded. "Let's give Minda and her friends a break. After all, they aren't used to coming to church or anything."

"Yeah!" Ben chimed in. "Give 'em a break!"

Everyone laughed at Ben's endearing way of mimicking everything they said.

"I think our youth group has some real possibilities if we all work hard at making it a comfortable, fun place for people to come and make friends and relax," Lexi said as she fixed root beer floats for everyone. "Not everyone has a home to come to and hang out like we do."

"You're right, Lexi," Binky agreed. "I guess we're pretty lucky."

"Right," Egg said, sipping on his root beer.

"Where else can you get food like we get here?"

———

The next evening, everyone gathered at the church for the Search for Christians party. No one knew what to expect, but being surprised was half the fun. Almost everyone wore jeans and a sweatshirt. Some had an extra sweater or jacket, and a hat—except for Minda and her friends, of course. They looked more like they were ready for a fashion show. Minda was decked out in leggings and a long sweater. Her blond hair was piled on her head, with a ponytail sticking out the top. She also wore huge dangling silver earrings.

Lexi was warm in her father's old hunting jacket, and Egg looked like a lumberjack in his plaid coat and billed cap with ear flaps.

Binky was giving Egg a hard time: "It's not that cold outside, Egg. Take off that goofy-looking hat."

"The Pastor said to wear something warm, if you recall. He also said we should wear hats. This is the only one I could find."

Binky rolled her eyes. "Even Dad doesn't wear that hat anymore. It's too stupid looking."

"My head's warm, okay?"

Pastor Lake clapped his hands to quiet the room. He stood in the middle of the group with a broad grin on his face. "Before we leave the church, I'd like to explain a little about the Search for Christians game."

"We're going to leave the church?" someone gasped.

"Where are we going?" another asked.

"We're going to Brian James' farmhouse," he answered simply.

Brian was a quiet boy who attended the church regularly.

"Before we leave, I'll assign your roles."

"Is this a play or something?" someone asked.

"You could call it that," Pastor Lake acknowledged. "We need to divide into two groups. Half of you on one side of the room, half on the other."

Noisily, everyone split up, some trying to stay close to their friends.

"The kids on this side of the room," Pastor Lake spoke loudly, and indicated the group Lexi was in, "are the Christians. The people on this side," he pointed to the others, which included Minda, "are the anti-Christians."

Egg snorted. "Seems fitting to me."

Binky poked him in the ribs. "Sh-h-h!"

"Now, let's all get into the vans waiting outside. There will be a flashlight for each of you. When we get to the James' farm, I'll explain the rest of the game."

Everyone eagerly climbed into the vehicles. Pastor Lake had captured their interest. The ride was brief, and a cheer rose when they pulled up in front of the attractive white farmhouse.

"Okay, here's how it works," Pastor Lake began when everyone had gathered outside the vans. "First, everyone take a good look at the farmhouse and where it is positioned among the other buildings and in relation to the fields. You need to be aware of its location because that is going to be our home base."

"Home base?" someone asked, puzzled.

A flurry of questions were raised in hushed tones throughout the group.

"Then, we will get into the vans again and be taken out to the fields." He gestured toward the ripened grain waving in the breeze. "You will be dropped off in various spots around the fields, with your flashlights and directions back to home base. The object is, that those of you who are the Christians have to find your way back to home base without being waylayed by the enemy—the anti-Christians.

"Those of you who are the anti-Christians are to do everything you can to keep the Christians from returning to home base. Is that clear to everyone?"

"I don't get it. What's the point?" Minda snapped her gum and struggled to look bored.

"When we as Christians travel through life to home base—heaven, or the safety and security of God's arms—we have a lot of rough territory to cover. There are obstacles to face, and an enemy to overcome.

"You see, Satan and his forces don't want the Christian to overcome and arrive safely home," Pastor Lake explained. "It takes faith and perseverance. Often the Enemy uses other people to hinder our progress, to tempt us away from God. This little game is a graphic demonstration of how Christians have to keep their eyes fixed on their Goal in order to avoid dangers in their path."

"So, we're supposed to try to catch as many of these Christians as we can?" Gina asked.

"Exactly. You can bring them to the holding pen." Pastor Lake pointed to a small pigpen with two pigs snuffling happily in their trough. "After a predetermined time, we'll count to see how many Christians actually made it home."

"And then we'll know how many fell by the wayside and ended up with the pigs, right?" Egg asked gleefully, rubbing his hands together. "This sounds like fun!"

"After we've counted the harvest on both sides, Brian's mother will have a good snack for us. The Christians who have made it home will be served first. Appropriate, don't you think?"

Everyone was beginning to relax and enjoy the prospect of the game. It wasn't as hard as some had imagined, and actually sounded like a lot of fun.

Minda was already plotting her strategy with Gina and Tressa. They were whispering furtively together.

"Okay, is everyone ready to get in the vans again and be scattered?" the pastor asked.

A cheer arose. "All right, now remember, only use your flashlight when it is absolutely necessary. Keep your eye on the house—the goal—and have fun."

As they piled into the vans, everyone babbled excitedly. Egg was planning his course. It was hard for him not to give away his strategy.

"I don't want to be dropped off alone," Binky whimpered. "I'm not smart enough or strong enough."

"Maybe we can all go together," Lexi suggested, indicating Peggy and Jennifer.

"What about me?" Egg suddenly felt left out. "I don't feel close to the other guys. Without Todd I'm kinda lost."

"Then come with us," Lexi said. "The van's stopping. Let's get out here."

The five found themselves standing in a field of tall grain. The porch light of the farmhouse could be seen in the distance, but it seemed like a long way away. The land, which had looked so flat from the farmyard, had become a series of gently rolling hills.

Lexi swallowed hard. "It's kind of scary, isn't it, to think that we're out here with nothing but flashlights and all those *anti-Christians* searching for us."

"It's kind of like life," Peggy said pensively. "Most of us have goals, whether it's to play first-string basketball, go to college, or simply reach a destination without being challenged or hindered along the way. But there are always obstacles. It's like Pastor Lake said, you just have to fix your eyes on the Goal and go for it."

This little game was beginning to make a lot of sense to Lexi. It was a parable of the Christian life. Everyone had problems to face now and then. Her problem right now was to make it safely to the distant porch light. Could she do it? Or would the forces of evil get in her way?

"Come on, guys. Let's go," Egg urged them on. "Let's give it a shot."

The ground was bumpier than any of them would have suspected. The furrowed rows of soft earth kept twisting their ankles. The golden wheat that had looked so soft in the fading light was stiff and bristly.

"I can't see where they dropped off any of the others. Can you?" Jennifer asked.

Egg, who'd scrunched down close to the ground, stood to take a look. Suddenly, a light flashed in his face and Tim Anders jumped out at him. "Gotcha! You're my captive now. You'll never make it to the light."

The girls dropped to their knees and remained still while Tim took his captive away.

"Poor Egg. He's going to have to sit in the pigpen until we all get back," Binky moaned. Then she grinned. "On the other hand, I think it might be good for him."

"Maybe we'd better spread out," Lexi suggested. "Otherwise, we'll all be captured at once."

They split up, stealthily working their way toward the farm house and the welcoming light.

After several close calls, Lexi finally reached the bright light over the farmhouse steps. It had been forty minutes. Binky and Peggy were already there.

"You made it, Lexi!" Peggy clapped. "Good for you."

"Is everyone else back?" Lexi asked, glancing around the farmyard.

"Almost," Binky answered. "I think there are only one or two who are still out."

"What about Jennifer?"

Peggy pointed toward the pigpen. Jennifer stood with Egg, a grim look on her face. A small pig nudged the back of her leg with his snout.

Lexi covered her mouth. It was hard not to giggle at the sight. "Did the anti-Christians catch many more?" she asked.

"Not as many as they wanted to. Minda was counting heads and bawling everyone out a few minutes ago.

Mrs. James opened the door and invited them inside for hot chocolate. When the last of the players had straggled in, Pastor Lake stood up, anxious to know if the game had been a success. "Well, what did you think of it?"

"Great!" the cheer was unanimous.

Even Minda acknowledged that it was fun.

"Did it make you think?" Pastor Lake asked.

A normally shy boy spoke up: "It made me think about the set-backs and problems Christians face. Every time I thought I had a free shot for the house, I saw someone moving through the field toward me. I had to stop and study where I was and ask myself if I was on the best path."

"Yeah," someone else agreed, "it reminded me of what my dad always says: how life is always regrouping, deciding if you're on the right track."

Pastor Lake's eyes sparkled at the insightful comments. "That's exactly right. I'm glad you were able to learn while having fun. Our road through life is just as difficult as the one we had to take tonight to make it to the safe haven on a dark night.

"Life is confusing and it doesn't come with a map. We have to make our way, seeking God's direction. Sometimes we get lost. Sometimes things or people get in our way and we have to go off in new directions, ones we hadn't planned."

"The thing I thought about," Jennifer volunteered, "is that it's not very easy being a Christian in an un-Christian world. The players who were anti-Christian seemed to be everywhere and the Christians were pretty hard to find. It seemed like we were outnumbered a hundred to one."

"Another good point," Pastor Lake commented. "Sometimes it *does* feel that way. That's why it's so important for those of us who are Christians to spend time together in fellowship and prayer. We can draw strength from each other to go on with our daily lives."

"It would have been easier," Egg said, "if we could have just knocked those anti-Christians over whenever they came near, but we weren't allowed to do that."

"That's right, Egg. We're required to act like Christians, like God's representatives in this world. Sometimes that's difficult."

"Humph!" Binky said loudly. "It isn't very easy being a Christian."

"That's also true," Pastor Lake agreed. "But the rewards are worth it."

When everyone was finished clearing up the snack, and had thanked Mrs. James for her hospitality, Pastor Lake stood to adjourn the evening. "Before we go home tonight, we have some business left over from our meeting last night. There was a question about the validity of the scheduled events. Would anyone like to see any changes?" Pastor Lake's eyes turned to Minda.

Everyone was quiet, a little uncomfortable with the question. They all recalled the reaction of Minda and her friends to the list of "childish games," as they called them. In the afterglow of the successful event they'd just participated in, Minda's ideas didn't seem so appealing.

Minda cleared her throat. "Why don't we just go ahead with the schedule as it stands, Pastor Lake." A flush seeped across her cheeks. "We can always make changes later, if necessary."

Several heads nodded in agreement. It'd taken a

great deal of courage for Minda to swallow her pride and admit that perhaps she hadn't been completely right after all.

"Good idea."

There would be no confrontation tonight to mar the happy atmosphere of the group.

The next afternoon, as Lexi put away her homework, she caught a glimpse of her grim reflection in the mirror. Though she still basked in the pleasure of the youth group night, right now she was dreading her visit to the hospital, and Todd.

"Lexi, I'm ready to leave for the grocery store. Do you want a ride?" Mrs. Leighton stepped into the doorway. She had a shopping bag on her arm. "You can visit Todd while I'm at the store."

"I suppose so. I'm almost ready."

"You don't sound very happy." Mrs. Leighton looked concerned. "Is something wrong?"

"Yes, Mother," Lexi blurted. She sank onto the bed. "Last time I was at the hospital, Todd was so terribly down he frightened me. I talked to Dad about it, and thought I was ready to face him again, but now the prospect of hearing him talk about how worthless he feels is depressing."

"I know, dear. I've talked to Todd's mother, and they're worried about him, too. He's been assigned a counselor now. Todd has been through a very traumatic time. We'll all just have to help him work things out."

"He's the only one who can work things out!" Lexi protested. "He's the one who has to choose life. He's the one who has to be convinced that his life is worth living. I never thought Todd would be the kind of coward that Chad Allan turned out to be."

"Give him time, Lexi. The accident was only days ago. Todd's feeling his way through his situation. His faith has been tested. That doesn't mean it's disappeared."

"I'll try to remember that," Lexi said grimly. "Even though it's hard."

When she left the elevator, Lexi took a deep breath to steady her nerves. She dreaded another encounter with Todd's sad face and discouraging words.

But when she stepped into his room, Lexi was surprised—shocked—to see Todd sitting in a wheelchair, his blond hair neatly combed, and a smile on his face.

"Hi, Lexi!" he greeted her cheerfully. "What's happening?"

"You're certainly looking better today!" she gasped.

"Yeah. They're letting me wear my own clothes, instead of that stupid hospital gown. I got a haircut, too. I needed one, don't you think?"

"It *was* getting kind of long."

"I considered a braid down the back, but decided it was too much trouble."

Lexi laughed. Todd laughed too. He was almost himself again. Lexi could hardly believe it. Something had happened—something good!

Chapter Seven

Lexi glanced around the hospital room. "You got a new poster!" She pointed to a hideous-looking creature that resembled a wart hog. It was peering into a mirror at its reflection. At the bottom of the poster were printed the words, "And you think *you've* got troubles!"

It was wonderful to see Todd's smile. "Jerry Randall brought that over. It's great, isn't it? He told me things could be a lot worse. I could look like *that* besides everything else!"

"Well, you're definitely in a good mood today," Lexi commented. "You're like a new person."

"It's the same old me, just a cheered-up version," Todd admitted.

"Is it because you're sitting up? I'm sure that helps. You really do look perfectly normal in the wheelchair," Lexi observed.

"I had a good report today," he said. "The doctors came in early this morning and had a long talk with me and my parents. I'm having a lot of sensation in my hands and feet. Better yet, I can wiggle my toes! Watch . . ."

Lexi leaned over as Todd scrunched up his face in

concentration. "Todd! They *are* moving. That's wonderful!"

"I can move my foot, too. The physical therapist says that if I continue to make progress, I'll be able to get my fingers around a glass soon. That's the first step toward eating at the Hamburger Shack, Lexi." Todd's eyes twinkled. "The doctors acknowledged that when I was brought in, the injury I had screamed *permanent*. But now, because the drug they gave me has decreased the swelling they can see that my spinal cord did not sustain permanent damage. I'm going to get better."

"Oh, Todd—" Lexi gasped.

"It'll be slow. The doctors and my therapist say it will still be discouraging at times, but I've decided that I'll do my part to recover as quickly as possible."

He paused thoughtfully. "Something else has happened since you were here last, Lexi."

"I guess you've been busy."

"Pastor Lake came again. We had a long talk about my accident. He's a great guy, isn't he?" Todd wore a lopsided grin. "Before I knew it, he had me telling him about how depressed I've been and how I'd been wondering if my life was worth anything. I even told him that I'd thought about ending my life, if I could find a way to do it."

At Lexi's look of consternation, Todd hastened to comfort her. "But I didn't really mean it, Lexi. I don't want to die. I don't think Chad did, either. Those are just stupid, destructive thoughts that play around in a person's mind when they're not fixed on God."

Todd stared out the window, his eyes focusing on something Lexi could not see.

"Pastor Lake really helped me understand things. I was feeling really sorry for myself—a cripple in a wheelchair. I assumed everyone pitied me. My parents, the doctors, you."

"That's not true, Todd."

"But that's what I thought. I can't stand pity, Lexi. It's humiliating. I didn't want that.

"What I really needed was to talk to someone who believed in miracles. Someone who could make me believe that possibly, just possibly, I could come out of this."

"And Pastor Lake was that person?"

"Yes, but he helped me to see that I can't be well until my mind is well, Lexi. I realize that now. Others can't help me do what I have to do for myself. Even if I never left this wheelchair, it doesn't mean I can't be a whole person.

"Pastor Lake showed me a verse in Job that says, 'Gird up your loins now, like a man.' He explained that was God telling Job when he was at his lowest point—full of sores and having lost everything—that it was time to get a grip on himself; to make some changes in his life; to start fresh. And the person you have to start with is yourself." His expression was full of new wisdom and understanding.

"That's where Chad made his mistake, Lexi. He blamed everyone else for what was wrong in his own life. He didn't look at himself and say, 'Hey, Chad, shape up. Start with yourself.' He pointed his finger at other people—especially Peggy. He wanted her to change. When he couldn't control her, he didn't want to live."

Todd's voice was confident and intense.

"The only person I have to control is *me*. If I'm going to get out of this wheelchair, I'm the one that has to work as hard as I possibly can in physical therapy. And even if I don't leave this chair, I'm the one who has to have the right attitude for staying in it. My life isn't over, Lexi. I was wrong when I thought that. But my life *is* changed. Even if I do get well, it's changed forever. I know things now that I never knew before. Do you know what I mean?"

Lexi nodded mutely. She was deeply touched by Todd's words.

"For a while, I thought God had abandoned me. But over the past couple of days, I've realized He hasn't. I started reading the book of Job. Now, *there's* a guy who had a tough time. He went from being a highly respected man to a man who was sick and pitied. When Job finally began to pull himself out of his predicament, he realized the help he needed all along was close at hand—God's help."

"It's so wonderful to hear you say that, Todd. I've prayed that you'd see that God was there for you—not just in the good times, but the bad times, too."

"I've always believed in God as the Creator of heaven and earth," Todd went on, "and that He knows when a sparrow falls from the sky, knows how many hairs are on our heads. God's a real 'detail' man. Now I've come to realize that this wheelchair can't be that big of a deal. If God wanted me out of it immediately, He could make it happen. Once I realized the kind of power I had on my side, I began to feel better."

"And you began to pray?"

"I was praying all the time. But I was afraid no one was listening."

"God has started listening now?" Lexi was trying to comprehend the marvelous change in Todd's attitude.

"Oh, He's been there all the time. He never leaves us. We're the ones who sometimes leave God. Pastor Lake reminded me that God *always* answers prayer. But He answers in His own time. I know now that I have to be patient. God will answer. I'm sure of it."

A smile brightened Todd's intense expression.

"As soon as I accepted that, Lexi, something happened to me. I didn't feel so frightened or defeated anymore. The only thing that changed was my attitude, but I felt better physically. Instead of belittling my mom when she looked for signs that I could move my hands and feet, I started paying attention to her. I started trying a little harder. And you know what? It happened."

Todd's eyes were moist. "I'm one of the lucky ones, Lexi. A lot of people try hard to recover and it never happens. But it's happening for me and I'm very thankful. And no matter to what degree I am healed, I know God will help me to live with it."

"So you're not angry anymore, Todd?" Lexi asked. "You had reason to be."

"That's what I thought. But it's over now. I realize anger won't better my situation, only make it worse." Todd's expression was regretful. "I've been really self-centered since this accident, Lexi. I haven't been nice to you, my mother, or the nurses. I know you all have my best interests at heart. So, I'm sorry, Lexi. I'm sure some days I'll get depressed, but if I remember that those times will pass, we'll all be better off." Todd's eyes twinkled. "I'll tell you to stay away on the bad days."

"You do that," Lexi said, with a relieved laugh. "I'll send Egg over."

"Good idea." Todd chuckled. "It's hard to be depressed with Egg around."

"You know, Todd, the change in you is like a miracle."

"I know. My mom's been praying for one—I'm sure she meant for my body, not my mind, though."

"Maybe that will come next," Lexi said hopefully.

"Who knows? At least now I feel I can handle it, whether it comes or not."

"Oh, Todd." Lexi put her arms around him and hugged him close. "Welcome back," she murmured.

In an effort to change the subject before his emotions got the best of him, Todd asked, "So, tell me what's going on at school, anything new?"

Lexi told him about the Search for Christians party and what a success it was. "We've decided to make it an annual event."

"I wish I could have been there. What did Minda and her gang think of it?"

"They had a great time, so much so, that Minda said she didn't see any reason to change the schedule of events for the year. The night before, she had made a big deal of the list, saying it was kids' stuff."

"That's great. So, I'll bet you're happy you invited them to join you, after all." Todd's expression changed. "How's Peggy doing?"

Lexi was pensive. "Peggy is pretty good. There are days when she is very positive and confident. But I think she still needs a lot of attention and close friendship to pull her through the days that are tough. Her moods are still erratic. Ever since your accident, I've spent less time with her, of course. Sometimes my heart aches for her, but I've been torn between being with her and being with you, to be honest."

"Sounds like Peggy needs you more right now than I do. I'm doing okay, as you can see. I feel better than I've felt in days."

Lexi smiled brightly. "And I'm so happy for you, Todd. Maybe I will check on Peggy right now."

"Of course, Lexi. I'll see you later. Don't worry about me."

———

Lexi left the hospital and went directly to Peggy Madison's home. Her parents were working on the lawn.

"Hi! Where's Peggy?" she called to them.

"Upstairs in her room, Lexi," her mother sighed, wiping her brow with her garden glove. "I'm sure she'd enjoy a visit from you."

Lexi let herself in the house and went upstairs to Peggy's room. She tapped lightly on the door.

"Who is it?" she asked faintly. It sounded like she'd been sleeping.

"It's me. Lexi. Did I wake you?"

"I guess so. Come on in, Lexi," came Peggy's weak reply.

"Are you tired?" Lexi asked.

"All the time. Lately, all I ever want to do is sleep," Peggy admitted. "Nothing else interests me."

Lexi had a hunch that it was easier to sleep than to try to pull herself out of her depression. "Let's go for a walk, Peggy," she offered. "The fresh air will do you good."

"You're probably right. I really need to talk to someone who understands me. My mom tries, Lexi, but I don't think she realizes that this thing takes time. I can't get over Chad's death just like that. I have to work through it. Does that make sense to you?"

"Of course it does, Peggy. Finally, I've got some good news for you. I've just come from the hospital. Todd's doing much better. His attitude has changed. He knows there will be days when he may feel depressed, but he is confident that God is with him and he can face whatever the outcome. He's doing much better physically, too. He was up in a wheelchair today."

"I'm glad to hear that, Lexi. I'm sure your prayers are being answered. I wish I had the kind of faith you have."

"You can have that faith too, Peggy!"

"I don't know, Lexi. I've done some pretty bad things in my life. I wonder if God can ever forgive me for all of it. I want to believe He can, but I'm just not sure."

"I know that He can and will, Peggy, but you have to believe it too. Jesus came to earth and died for sinners, not for people who think they've never done anything wrong."

"I never thought of it that way, Lexi. You always make everything sound so easy."

The girls walked and talked for another hour before they parted and went to their homes. Lexi mounted the stairs to the porch, glad that Todd was doing so much better, and that she'd been free to spend some valuable time with Peggy. When she was ready for bed she prayed for both of them. She was sure God had great things in store for all of them.

Chapter Eight

On Saturday afternoon, Lexi, Egg and Binky made their way to the rehabilitation section of the hospital, where Todd had been moved.

"It's been too long since we've seen Todd," Binky announced. "But we've had so much homework this week, Mom wouldn't let us out of the house."

When they reached Todd's room, the door was partially closed. Lexi tapped lightly. "Todd? Can we come in?"

"Of course. Come on." He was sitting in his wheelchair with a book propped in front of him.

"What are you up to?" Binky asked, seeing him out of bed for the first time.

"Studying. Is there anything you want to know about the French Revolution?"

"There's *nothing* I want to know about the French Revolution," Egg announced dramatically.

"You mean you even have to study while you're in the hospital?" Binky asked incredulously.

"You do if you want to keep up with your class," Todd said with a laugh. "I may be brilliant, but I do have to read the material, you know." He was moving his head more freely now and had regained some use of his arms and hands. Lexi thought he looked wonderful.

"You're moving around more than when I was here last," Egg said. "How's your therapy going?"

"Tiring. They work me non-stop."

Binky sighed heavily. "Oh, Todd, you're so brave. It must be really hard to go through that every day."

"It's not so bad. When I think about walking on my own again, the pain is worth it."

"I still think you're brave," Binky insisted.

"A lot more brave than Chad Allan was," Egg muttered under his breath.

There was an awkward silence. Todd was the first to speak.

"I'm sorry he didn't come to the realization of how precious life is. And it's scary to think how close I came to the frame of mind he must have been in before he died. But now, whatever condition I'm in, whether it's in a wheelchair, on crutches, or back to walking on my own, I know I want to live."

"That's the difference." Egg held his hands parallel to one another. "You and Chad lived your lives on separate tracks, running in the same direction. Both of you had bad things happen to you. Chad gave up and you didn't."

"To be honest, for a while I thought about giving up." Todd laughed dryly. "Problem was, I was too helpless to do anything about it. There was no way I could have taken my own life even if I'd really meant to. But I decided that if Chad was brave enough to commit suicide, he was brave enough to have chosen to live."

They were all silenced by Todd's somber words.

"Whatever movement or strength I get back, I'll take it with thankfulness. I really believe God is working in me. That's an exciting feeling."

Lexi could see that Binky and Egg were impressed with Todd's courage and faith. There *was* an ironic parallel between Chad's life and Todd's. Though they had traveled similar paths, their choices made all the difference.

Binky put her hand on Todd's arm. "Harry Cramer called last night. He asked how you were doing. I told him that I'd visit you today and give him a full report."

"Tell him hello for me. He's been great about sending me encouragement. I miss him." Todd looked frustrated. "I haven't mastered the use of a pencil yet, or I'd write to him myself."

"Lexi says it won't be long, though," Egg offered hopefully, his eyes riveted on Todd's hands.

"She's right. I am progressing with the physical therapy. I'm exhausted when we're through, and I think the therapists are too. It's a lot of work getting my limbs to move again."

"Does that mean you'll be walking soon?" Binky couldn't help but ask.

"I wish that were true. It could be weeks, months, no one knows for sure. Everyone responds differently to therapy."

Binky nodded, trying to look optimistic. It was hard for her "now" personality to wait.

"We're praying that it will be soon, Binky," Lexi hurried to say.

"I'm feeling a lot more hopeful than I was. Although my faith doesn't depend on the final outcome,

I do think I'll walk again, Binky."

"I'm going to tell Harry that," Binky decided. She crossed her thin arms over her chest. "He's discovered that being a college man isn't as easy as he thought it was going to be. He signed up for eighteen credits and now he's swamped. He says he wishes he were back at Cedar River High School where all the classes were a 'piece of cake.' "

"A piece of cake?" Egg snorted. "Hah! My chemistry class is no piece of cake. Harry Cramer doesn't know what he's talking about."

Binky glared at her brother, but left it at that. She didn't want to start an argument in a hospital room.

Todd was quick to change the subject. "It's great to see you guys. I've realized for the first time just how important my friends are, and more particularly, *who* they are. Some people I expected to visit haven't come." He sighed. "I really thought Matt Windsor would have been in to see me."

Lexi sank down on a chair across from Todd, and met her eyes with his. "I've talked to Matt about it, Todd. He said he's been afraid to come up to the hospital. He doesn't want to see you lying in bed helpless. He's scared. Lots of the kids are."

"But I'm not in bed and I'm not helpless. I'm the same person I was before the accident!"

"I know, Todd. I told him that. I think he'll come yet. He said he knows it could have been him instead of you, riding his motorcycle and all. Another thing is, a lot of people don't like to be around someone who's sick or hurt." Lexi cleared her throat. "I should know that better than anyone, having Ben for a brother. People are uncomfortable around defects and imperfections. It reminds them that they're vulnerable, too."

Lexi could see Todd relax. After a few moments, as they all stood to leave, Matt Windsor stepped into the room.

"Hey, man, we were just talking about you! Come on in."

"Hi, everybody. You don't have to leave just because I came."

"No, but we've been here awhile. You two need some time alone," Lexi said, smiling.

"It was great to see you," Egg said on the way out.

"More than great. It was wonderful." Binky leaned over and gave Todd a big smack on the cheek. When she stood up, there was an impish grin on her face. "I've always wanted to do that."

"You didn't have to wait for a catastrophe to happen first," Todd said.

"Bye, Todd." Lexi gave him a quick kiss on the forehead.

The three made their way down the hospital corridor and out into the fresh air.

Binky walked backward across the hospital lawn. Her eyes were shining. "Doesn't Todd look wonderful?"

Lexi smiled. "He looks like himself again. For a while I thought he would never be the same again."

Binky's eyes turned misty. "I've never met anyone so brave in my entire life. I couldn't be that happy sitting in a wheelchair."

"Yeah," Egg said. "It's not my idea of a fun place

to be. Just when he was making it as our quarter-back. It was a tough break all right."

"Well, Todd has a reason to be happy, you know," Lexi said.

"I know, I know." Binky held up her hand. "It's his faith. Todd believes in God."

"That's what's getting him through this."

Binky's expression was wistful. "It would be nice to have faith like that." She turned to her brother. "Wouldn't it, Egg?"

Lexi could practically hear the wheels turning in Egg's head. "Frankly, I never thought I'd be saying this, but in a way, I envy Todd."

"You do?" Lexi looked surprised.

"I can't even begin to imagine having so much faith that you'd be able to smile while strapped in a wheelchair," Egg said bluntly.

"Have you ever wanted to have faith like that, Egg?" Lexi asked him.

Egg looked at her with a pained expression. "I'm not like Todd, Lexi. I didn't grow up in a home where God and religion were subjects of conversation. When I was little, the only time I ever heard the Lord's name was . . ." Egg blushed until his ears turned pink. ". . . as a swear word."

"That doesn't matter, Egg. God doesn't judge you by what kind of background you come from. He wants you to come to Him as you are, questions and all."

Before Egg could answer, they looked up to see Pastor Lake walking toward them.

"Hi, kids. What's new?"

They relayed to him the good visit they'd just had

with Todd. "He's doing so much better since you talked with him," Lexi said.

"That's good to hear," Pastor Lake said, beaming. "I'm glad I could be of some encouragement. Maybe at our next youth meeting, we could all work on a homemade card for Todd and have everyone sign it. It'll be great when he's well enough to join us."

Lexi was glad the young pastor sounded so confident of Todd's full recovery.

"Frankly, I need someone to help me with the next meeting," Pastor Lake said finally. "Do you think you could help me? We'll need some prizes and some food."

"Oh, I'd love to fix the food," Binky said. "We could have tacos or sloppy joes or . . ."

"How many prizes will we need?" Egg interrupted.

"Five, and then five more booby prizes. Do you think you can handle that?"

"Sure! What are the prizes for?"

"One of the ideas on the list was a scavenger hunt. How does that sound?"

"Great! We'll talk about prizes at the Hamburger Shack. We're on our way there right now."

"Thank you, guys. See you later." Pastor Lake waved to them as he turned the corner and headed for the church.

"He sure is nice, isn't he?" Binky said. "I think the youth group is a lot of fun, Lexi. It's made me want to go to church more often."

When they arrived at the Hamburger Shack, they found their places at the back of the room. Binky pulled out a pencil and began writing on a napkin.

"If no one has a complaint, I think we should have tacos," she announced. "We could slice and dice everything at home. And they'd be really easy to serve. How does that sound?"

"Sounds good to me," Egg said, licking his lips.

Binky began listing ingredients on the napkin. "Shall I ask some of the kids to help bring some of the stuff?"

"Sure, Binky, but that's the easy part," Egg said. "We've got to think of prizes. We want them to be special."

Binky sighed and shook her head. "Egg wants to eat, but he never thinks there's any work to it."

"What's this I hear about prizes?" The owner of the Hamburger Shack, Mr. Ingall, walked over to their booth. He was a big man with broad shoulders and an ample stomach. His size hinted that he enjoyed his own cooking. "Are you having a contest or something?"

The three explained about the scavenger hunt their youth group was having.

"Sounds like a worthy cause to me. I could provide some prizes for you."

"You could?" Egg was flabbergasted. "What kind of prizes?"

"I could give you some gift certificates for use here at the Shack, say for a banana split, milkshake, hamburger and fries?"

"Yum-m-m. What a terrific idea!" Binky enthused.

"Thanks, Mr. Ingall," Egg said.

"We really appreciate your generosity," Lexi added.

"Good, glad to hear it. In fact, here's another idea: The top winner will get a certificate for free after-school snacks for a week. How does that sound?"

Lexi could see Egg beginning to drool. He didn't have a lot of money, and snacks and meals at the Hamburger Shack were always a strain on his finances.

"Now I know what the word motivation means," Egg said. "I'm *very* motivated to win that prize."

"Tell Jerry Randall he's invited to come to our youth meeting Friday night," Lexi said. "I think it's going to be a lot of fun."

Jerry's boss laughed. "I'll tell him, but I'm not sure he'll think treats from the Hamburger Shack are much of a prize."

Chapter Nine

For Lexi, the days were passing more quickly now. Since Todd's attitude had changed, his therapy grew more intensive and his days busier.

At school, all the teachers seemed to have joined in a pact to assign as much homework as possible each evening.

The date for the scavenger hunt was upon them before they knew it. Lexi and her friends could hardly contain their excitement as they descended the stairs to the church basement. If everything went according to plan, this would be a very eventful evening.

The room was packed with young people. Tim Anders and Mary Beth Adamson were having a dispute over the rules of shuffleboard in a far corner of the room. Anna Marie Arnold was engaged in conversation with Pastor Lake. Someone was pounding away on the slightly off-key piano—the rhythm punctuated by the sound of corn popping.

Lexi noticed Peggy Madison, through the large kitchen serving window, stirring a pitcher of lemonade. Egg was making his usual rounds, lifting lids and peeking under aluminum foil at the plates of goodies. Binky stalked behind him, slapping his fingers and reprimanding him.

In spite of Binky's bird-like hovering, Egg managed to steal two brownies before she pounced on him.

Minda Hannaford sprawled lazily on a lounge chair. Lexi had to chuckle at Minda's efforts to get Matt Windsor's attention by batting her long eyelashes. But the more she flirted, the more furious Jennifer Golden's expression grew. Jennifer managed to stand at a convenient distance for eavesdropping. Her face became redder by the minute and her blue eyes flashed. Lexi could see a storm brewing. She suppressed a grin. Everything was as calm, orderly, and normal as it was ever going to get!

Pastor Lake broke away from his conversation with Anna Marie and clapped his hands loudly. "I'd like to call this meeting to order, please, so that we can get our scavenger hunt underway."

Clapping and cheering arose from the crowd.

"Before we begin, let's ask God to bless this evening's activities:

"Dear Heavenly Father, bless our fellowship here tonight. Help us to realize how important the gift of friendship is. Encourage us to treat each other with respect and courtesy, keeping in mind who our very Best Friend is.

"Keep us safe tonight, Lord. In our searching about the town, help us to remember that we are representatives of You. We ask this in Jesus' name, Amen."

Pastor Lake raised his head, and a broad smile lit his face. All eyes were on him.

"First of all," he began, "we'll divide into groups of five. Each group will receive an identical list of items to search for. Find as many of these items as you possibly can, in homes, stores, wherever. The group who finds all the items listed will be the winner, and each member will receive a prize. The group coming in second will receive lesser prizes."

"What're the prizes?" Tressa asked, with a long pout on her face.

"A week's worth of after-school snacks at the Hamburger Shack for the team with all the items, and gift certificates for the second-place winners. It'll be worth your energy and effort, don't you think?"

Tressa nodded silently.

"Remember that you represent our church, and more specifically, Jesus Christ. Act in a polite, gracious manner. If you find an item that the owner is not willing to part with, please do not bribe them. Is that clear?"

A moan went up from the High-Fives. "No bribing?"

"You will have an hour and a half to find the items on your list. Everyone must return to the church at that time, whether or not you are finished."

"What if you have just one thing left, and you know where it is?" Tim Anders asked.

"Come back to the church anyway. I suppose we could search all night for a black key-chain or a lock of red hair, but we have to have a deadline."

"I have a black key-chain!" somebody piped.

"And I have red hair!" hooted one of the girls.

"Sorry, folks," Pastor Lake chuckled. "Neither of those items are on the list. It might be good to begin in your own homes, then try the homes of neighbors and friends, and strangers as a last resort. Wherever you think you can find the items on the list is fair game. Remember to explain your purpose and don't be rude or demanding."

"We're ready!" Matt Windsor blurted. "Let's get started."

"Okay, number off: one, two, three, four, five . . . Form your groups, and grab a list from the table. Have fun!"

Lexi was pleased to see that Binky was in her group. Then Minda and Jerry joined them, and Joe, a newcomer.

"You're with us?" Binky asked incredulously.

"I'm not happy about it, either," Minda retorted. Jerry scowled.

Reading their mood, Pastor Lake said, "You may not be in the group you came with tonight, but the idea is to meet others. We can make friends while we have fun. Everyone is equal in the Family of God; let's show some love and consideration."

Binky was obviously embarrassed, and Minda nodded her head grudgingly.

Egg and Matt Windsor were in a group with Anna Marie Arnold, Tim Anders, and a new girl. Jennifer Golden was paired with Tressa and three others Lexi didn't know.

It would have been more fun, Lexi mused, *if our own gang could have worked together as a group. We did solve the mystery of the kidnapped tennis player this summer.* In spite of her thoughts, Lexi understood the Pastor's desire that everyone mingle. Cliques had no place in the church. Everyone was the same in God's eyes.

Vowing to make the best of it, Lexi turned to Minda with a hopeful smile. Minda crossed her arms over her chest, and pressed her lips in a thin line.

Binky grabbed the list for their group. "I want us to win first prize. I'm always broke, and this way I can have real food all week at the Hamburger Shack—for free! All we have to do is find this stuff."

Jerry, Joe, and Lexi moved a step closer to peer at the list. Even Minda, although she tried to act disinterested, craned her neck in an attempt to see the items.

"A blue racquet ball, a music stand, a philodendron, a cherry danish, a pair of Mickey Mouse ears, a black golf tee . . ." Binky's voice trailed away. "We could be at this all night."

"We only have an hour and a half, remember?" Lexi said.

There were whoops, groans and complaints coming from the other groups.

"This is too hard," someone moaned.

"Where are we going to find a socket wrench?"

"The Chinese restaurant is closed for remodeling," someone else informed them. "How can we find a fortune cookie?"

Pastor Lake held up his arm and looked at his watch. "You have one more minute before we begin. Stay together in your groups. If you have access to a car, you may use it. Remember to go to each stop together. The first group to find everything on the list and return to the church is the winner. On your mark, get set—go!"

Minda gave Jerry a shove in the small of his back. "We're outta here!"

Jerry blinked twice and headed for the stairs.

They made their way into the church parking lot. Cars were already speeding away. Three groups had taken off on foot. Binky, who was clutching the scavenger list, continued to peer at it with her brows furrowed together.

"A blue racquet ball. That shouldn't be too hard. Do any of you play racquetball?" she looked anxiously from Jerry to Minda.

"Not me," Jerry shrugged his shoulders. "Who has time?"

"The logical place to find it is at the racquetball club," Minda said, with an air of authority. "I've got my car. I'll drive."

They piled into Minda's car and she peeled out of the parking lot with a swerving screech. Lexi bit her lower lip and buckled her seat belt. Maybe this scavenger hunt thing wasn't such a good idea after all—not if everyone got so excited they ended up in an accident.

"What else is on the list?" Minda demanded. "Anything we can pick up along the way to the club?"

"Does anyone have a music stand?"

"There are dozens of them at the school," Lexi offered. "But that's locked up for the night."

"Who do we know who uses a music stand at home?" Binky asked.

"Who do we know that practices at home?" Minda snorted.

Jerry snapped his fingers. "I've got it! My aunt plays the flute. She has a music stand in her family room. I'm sure she'd let us use it."

"Is it anywhere near the racquetball club?"

Minda asked, glancing at her watch. "We haven't got much time, you know."

"A couple of blocks away."

"Good. We'll stop there as soon as we get the ball." Minda careened into the sports club parking lot.

"Oh, no . . ." Jerry groaned. "They're closed."

A large wooden sign posted across the door said: *Closed for Renovations.*

"There's a light inside," Joe said.

"Probably a janitor."

"Now what are we going to do?"

"We're not giving up." Minda parked the car and jumped out. "Help!" she called. "Please, let us in!"

A heavy-set man in a tight T-shirt came to the door and peered through the glass. "What do you want?"

"I need a blue racquet ball. Do you have one?"

He opened the door a crack. "We're closed."

"We need it tonight. Can you help us?"

"You can't play racquetball here. I can't give you a ball, if you don't use it here."

Binky held the scavenger hunt list up. "We'd bring it back in a couple of hours."

"For some stupid game, huh?"

"We're from the youth group at the Good Shepherd Community Church. We're having a scavenger hunt. Do you have a blue ball?" Binky danced around on tiptoe.

He scowled first at Binky, then Minda. Lexi and the boys stayed in the background.

"I shouldn't be doing this," he growled, but the door glided open. "There might be some dead ones behind the desk. Come on."

Minda and Binky disappeared into the building. They emerged a few moments later, triumphant. "We've got it! Check it off the list."

They jumped into the car, and Minda pulled out of the parking lot, making a beeline for the next stop.

They didn't have to beg this time. Jerry's aunt willingly turned over her music stand with the admonition to bring it back as soon as they were done. Jerry carefully folded it and put it in the trunk of the car.

"Oh, wait!" Binky yelped. "We have to have a philodendron. Does your aunt have one of those?"

"What's a philodendron?" Jerry looked at her blankly. "Sounds like some kind of medication."

"It's a plant, silly. It has big green leaves shaped like hearts."

"I don't know. She's got some plants in there."

"Go find out!" Binky pushed him out of the car. Jerry reluctantly dragged himself back inside.

"I wish he'd hurry up," Minda moaned. "We're getting behind."

Momentarily, Jerry returned, his arms full of plants.

"Not every plant in the house! Just the philodendron."

"Well, I couldn't remember what it was called," he said. "Here, you pick it out." He thrust the plants toward Binky.

Minda and Lexi searched through African violets, spider plants, and grape ivy. A small philodendron was propped in the crook of Jerry's arm, and Lexi plucked it out.

"Take the rest back to your aunt and tell her thanks."

Once they were in the car again with the philodendron perched on Binky's lap, Minda asked, "Now what?"

"A Los Angeles Kings hockey sweatshirt," Lexi read from the list. "Who in the world would have one of those?"

"I know a guy who'd have one for sure," Jerry said.

He and Joe looked at each other and said the name simultaneously: "Max Fischer."

"Who's Max Fischer?" Binky wondered.

"The biggest L.A. Kings hockey fan in Cedar River," Jerry said. "The sporting goods stores are closed, so if Max Fischer doesn't have one, we aren't going to find one."

Following Jerry's directions, Minda drove directly to the home of Max Fischer. It was a small bright blue rambler. Ceramic statues of Snow White and the Seven Dwarfs paraded across the neatly kept lawn.

"This is where Max Fischer lives?" Binky sounded doubtful. "Are you sure he'll have a sweatshirt?"

"Positive."

Everyone piled out of the car. Lexi was curious. She wanted to meet this Max. But before Binky could press the bell, the door opened.

"Don't tell me. Let me guess," said a thin, dark-haired man with wire-rimmed glasses. "You want an L.A. Kings sweatshirt, right?"

"You mean somebody's already been here?" Jerry groaned.

"Somebody? About twenty people. It's been like Grand Central Station all night."

"Oh, no!" Binky pounded the heel of her hand against her forehead. "We've lost." She sat on the steps, already in despair.

Max stared at the pathetic sight. "What's wrong with her?"

"She likes to win," Lexi explained sheepishly. She poked Binky with the toe of her shoe. "Get up," she whispered.

"I hate losing! Especially to my brother! Egg McNaughton is the one who got your sweatshirt, right?"

"Afraid so," the tall man admitted. "This really means a lot to you, doesn't it, kid?"

"I'll never hear the end of it. Never! My life is ruined." Binky, always given to dramatics, could have won an Academy Award for this one.

A frown crossed Max's face. "Well, they really only got my good one."

Binky's ears perked up. "Your *good* one? You mean you have an old one?"

"Yeah. Just a rag I use for painting around the house."

Binky jumped to her feet and grabbed the front of his shirt. "I don't care if it's in bad shape. I'll take it. I don't care if it's covered with paint. I'll even bring it back clean—I promise!"

The man looked at Binky as if she'd lost her mind. "You don't have to bring it back. You can have it. Just a minute, I'll see if I can find it."

Binky jumped up and down, whooping and hollering. She flung her arms around Minda and whirled the startled girl in circles.

"You get full credit for this one, Binky," Minda conceded. "If it hadn't been for that big production, he'd never have thought of his old L.A. Kings sweat-shirt."

In a moment Max returned, the stained shirt in hand. The sleeves had been cut off unevenly, and it was stiff with paint, but the L.A. Kings logo was still legible.

"Don't bring it back!" he ordered. "I don't want to see it again." Somehow, the others got the feeling Max didn't want to see Binky again either.

"Thank you, thank you, thank you! A million thanks." Binky pressed the shirt to her chest.

Max Fischer shook his head. "No problem. You win the prize for being the most persistent." He closed the door abruptly.

The five returned to their car. Jerry glanced at the list and sank into his seat. "I don't know what we're so excited about, we can't win this game any-way."

"What's next?" Minda demanded, undaunted.

"Where are we going to find a pink carnation this time of night?"

"I've got one!" Lexi shouted. "My dad gave my Mom flowers two days ago. I'm sure there are car-nations in the bouquet."

"Is there anything else on the list we could find at your house?" Binky asked, her excitement mount-ing.

Lexi scanned the sheet. "My dad plays golf. He might have a black golf tee."

Arriving at her home, Lexi ran inside to collect

the carnation while Minda and the others sifted through Dr. Leighton's golf bag in the garage. When she came out, they had golf tees scattered all over the floor.

"There's not a black one in the lot," Minda complained.

"Maybe they don't even make black tees. I'll bet they don't!" Binky squawked. "How can we find something that doesn't exist?"

Lexi thought hard for a moment, staring at the multicolored array of tees. "If they don't exist, maybe we could *make* one!" She scanned the shelf containing car wax and paint cans. "There's a spray can of black paint here . . . somewhere."

"Great idea!" Jerry spread some old newspaper on a bench, while Lexi found the paint.

"Let's paint two!" Binky said, tossing a second tee onto the paper.

"What do we want two for?"

Binky's eyes twinkled. "Maybe we could sell one—even if we don't make first prize, maybe we could make a little cash on the side."

Minda chuckled. "Binky McNaughton, you surprise me."

Binky grinned. "I surprise myself sometimes."

They were all laughing as they drove to Minda's to collect a colander, an out-dated phone book, Mickey Mouse ears, and a pair of size eight tennis shoes. Then they made a quick stop at the grocery store to get a fortune cookie and a cherry danish.

"We still don't have a socket wrench," Binky moaned.

"Hey, Todd's brother, Mike, would have one," Lexi

said excitedly. "He's a mechanic!"

"Let's go!" Minda shouted, racing through the grocery store parking lot to get to her car.

After borrowing Mike's wrench, they all collapsed breathlessly into Minda's car and checked the last item off their list.

"Our time's almost up," Jerry said. "We'd better get back to the church."

"And we have it all. Let's go!"

"Step on it, Minda!" Binky could hardly contain herself. Minda glanced at Binky as she bounced up and down in the front seat. "I'm not going to get in a car wreck over a stupid scavenger hunt, McNaughton."

"Oh." Binky deflated against the seat. "Sorry. I get so excited."

"It's okay, I understand. You're my kind of person," Minda mumbled.

The oddly formed group had warmed to one another. They'd actually had *fun*.

Jerry pointed out the window. "There's Jennifer's group. They're coming in, too. We've got to beat 'em. Quick! Gather the stuff."

"Jerry, you get the music stand. Binky, be careful of the philodendron," Lexi ordered.

They scrambled out of the car and raced through the church doors. "We made it! We made it! We beat 'em! We're first! We're first . . ." Binky droned.

The words died on her lips as they entered the church basement. Egg and his group were sitting calmly at a table, drinking hot chocolate. The table in front of them was piled high with their catch—a blue racquet ball, the L.A. sweatshirt, a large and decrepit-looking philodendron. There was even a black golf tee.

"You're here already?" the girls gasped together. Egg and his crew smirked confidently. "We've been here for ages."

"You cheated!" Binky yelped.

"We did not! We just happened to know where to find things, that's all."

"I bet you don't have it all." She stomped over to the table and looked through the loot. "Hey! Where'd you get this phone book?" Binky glared at her brother. "You took it out of my bedroom, didn't you?"

"It was the only *old* phone book we could find. *Most* people throw away such things."

"You had no right to go into my bedroom," Binky whined. "You know you have to ask my permission."

"I thought you wouldn't mind just this once. After all, it was a special occasion."

"I *especially* don't want you to go into my bedroom on special occasions!" Binky shouted, her hands on her hips and her jaw thrust out in a defiant manner. "I don't go into *your* room. We would have won if you hadn't been able to get my phone book."

Almost everyone had returned by now, and all eyes were on Binky and Egg as they squared off.

Lexi could see that Pastor Lake was trying to suppress a chuckle. He walked over to the pair and put a hand on each of their shoulders. "I think you both did very well."

Binky still wore a pout. "Since Egg's team wins, I think our group should at least be first in line for the food tonight."

"But, Binky, your group will get second-place prizes!"

"Oh, yeah. I almost forgot," she said, giving up the fight.

"Why don't we have a brief prayer of thanks before we eat?" Pastor Lake bowed his head.

"Dear Heavenly Father, thank you for this great evening of fun. Thank you for the new friendships made tonight. We ask your special blessing and presence with Todd Winston, Father. We miss him and trust that he will soon be back with us—healed and walking. Help us to remember how precious life is, Lord, that we might cherish every moment of it. Amen.

"Binky McNaughton has made tacos for all of us. Others have brought desserts. Enjoy!" Pastor Lake extended an arm and announced, "First- and second-place winners, lead the way."

When most of them had their food and were sitting, Lexi sensed a new feeling of warmth and fellowship in the room. Many had gathered into clusters and were visiting quietly, some with new friends they'd met only this evening. Binky and Minda were having a congenial conversation at one table; Jerry Randall was listening in, occasionally offering a word or two of his own. It was amazing, really, the barriers that had been broken down throughout the evening.

As Lexi headed for home, she felt light-hearted and happy. For the first time in many weeks, she felt genuine hope. Todd was getting feeling back in his hands and legs. The youth group was off to a good start. An invisible wall had broken down between Binky and Minda.

Yes, indeed, miracles did happen!

Chapter Ten

Lexi was doing her homework at the kitchen table when the telephone rang. "Hello. Leightons'. Lexi speaking."

"Hello, Lexi. This is Mrs. Winston. I'm calling about Todd."

"Is he all right? Is everything okay?"

Mrs. Winston's ready laugh soothed Lexi immediately. "Everything's fine, Lexi. In fact, things are quite wonderful. I just wanted to let you know that Todd is being transferred from the rehab section of the hospital to the rehabilitation center down the road."

"He is? That's good news, isn't it?"

"Very good. He's been making great progress. So well, in fact, the doctors have decided the best place for him is the rehab center. They have more sophisticated equipment there than at the hospital. They're going to start him on the parallel bars right away."

"Parallel bars?"

"Todd will stand by himself with only the support of the bars at his sides. Once he's mastered walking between the bars he'll graduate to a walker."

"And then?" Lexi held her breath.

"From the walker, he'll go to crutches, and then to a cane." Mrs. Winston's voice broke. "Oh, Lexi. He's going to be walking again! It's happening faster than anyone anticipated. Our worst fears are over. Of course, Todd thinks his improvement is slow, but the doctors say it's as rapid as anyone could expect."

There were tears streaming down Lexi's cheeks. "He's really going to walk again! Oh, Mrs. Winston, I'm so happy, so relieved."

"We all are."

"When can I see him next?"

"He's going to be kept very busy at the rehabilitation center. The classes and physical therapy sessions are quite intense. Actually, they recommend only the immediate family visit until he is accustomed to the new schedule and staff. Why don't you wait a few days, Lexi."

"Would Saturday be all right?"

"Saturday would be fine. The weekend will be less hectic for him. I'm sure he'd love to see you then."

Saturday. Will it ever come?

Somehow, Lexi managed to get through the week without losing her mind. She knew her attention span in class had been limited, and the Emerald Tones had to put up with her delayed entrance and off-key harmony, but it didn't matter. Todd was getting better, and she was going to see him on Saturday.

She arose early and showered leisurely. It was only eight o'clock when she went downstairs. No one was around yet, so she went outside to take in the crisp fall air.

The leaves were beginning to turn color after an

early frost. Lexi loved the change of the seasons. Nature was never boring with its palette of beautiful colors—pastel spring flowers and green grass, autumn's red, yellow, and golden hues, the crystalline white of winter.

Lexi noticed happily that there were some marigolds and zinnias still left in the garden. She spotted her mother's shears and cut a bouquet for Todd. When she returned to the kitchen, Mrs. Leighton was preparing breakfast.

"Those are lovely, Lexi. Are they for Todd?"

"Do you have a vase I could use?"

"Sure. There're several in the small cupboard above the broom closet. Take whatever you like. And remember to take that box on the table. I packed some goodies for him."

"Mom, that's sweet of you. I'm afraid he's going to get spoiled, though. Last time I brought some of your cookies, he complained that he was going to get fat."

"Oh? He ate them, didn't he?" Mrs. Leighton smiled.

"Of course, Mom. I've never known Todd to turn down a good cookie."

"I thought so. I can't imagine Todd being really worried about gaining weight. He can always send the cookies back if he doesn't want them."

They were laughing together when Ben came bounding down the stairs in his pajamas. He looked like he'd only been awake a few seconds.

"Are you going to see Todd now?" he asked eagerly.

"I haven't had breakfast yet. I've been waiting for you, sleepyhead."

"Ben's ready," he said with a big grin. "And you can't go until I give you my present for Todd."

"Everybody wants to send something to Todd."

"That's because he's getting well!" Ben said with enthusiasm. He turned around and disappeared into the living room. A moment later he returned clutching a sheaf of papers. "These are pictures. I drew them for Todd. Aren't they be-ooo-tiful?"

Lexi spread the wrinkled sheets on the table. There was a picture of a big blue car, obviously depicting Todd's '49 Ford Coupe. Another was of a large brick building with a maintenance bay. Two men stood in the small doorway and a car was pulled into the bay.

"This must be Mike's garage," Lexi guessed.

"Right!"

The other pictures were Ben's renditions of his world—his bunny in the backyard hutch, his swing set, and the Academy.

"Todd will love these, Ben. Thank you."

————

Lexi parked at the rehab center and made her way to the reception desk. Learning the directions to Todd's new room, she started down the hall, her stomach fluttering with a twinge of nervousness. She hadn't seen him for a few days, even though they'd talked on the phone every evening. He often sounded exhausted. The therapy was very demanding.

Her hands full, she tapped on the door with her foot.

"Come in."

Todd was sitting in a wheelchair next to the window, wearing jeans and a pale blue shirt. Lexi never could get over how bright his eyes looked when he wore blue. His blond hair was falling loosely on his forehead. He smiled broadly at Lexi when she stepped into the room.

He looks marvelous! Lexi thought.

"I've been waiting for you! You must have parked on the other side. I've been watching the parking lot for nearly half an hour."

Lexi thrust out her arms with the gifts. "I'm sorry. Everyone had something to send you. The flowers are from me, Mother sent the goodies, and Ben drew you some pictures."

Todd whistled. "Where do I start?"

"How about a cookie. They always seem to be your favorite."

Lexi was surprised to see Todd reach for the box and take it from her.

"Todd!" she gasped. "You're using both your arms!"

"I know. Isn't it great? The doctors are pleased with my progress. Can you get the lid off this thing for me?"

"Sure. Do you have any scotch tape? I'll hang up Ben's pictures."

By the time she'd hung the pictures and arranged the flowers on the bedside table, Todd had devoured nearly half the goodies Mrs. Leighton sent.

"Tell your mother to make more of this stuff," he said. "Tell her the doctors have prescribed it. It's bound to get me walking sooner."

Lexi laughed. "Yeah, right. How's it going?" Lexi

was almost afraid to ask. "Are you, uh—walking yet?"

"Push that walker over here and I'll show you."

Lexi moved a lightweight aluminum walker to Todd's wheelchair. He centered it in front of the chair, and grasping it firmly, slowly propelled himself to a standing position.

"Todd!" Lexi gasped. "I can't believe it."

"Neither could my physical therapist." He grinned delightedly. "My goal is to be out of here weeks before anyone believed possible."

He dropped back into the wheelchair. "That may not be an impressive display of strength, considering how strong I used to be, but it's a start. I'm so tired of hospitals, rehab, doctors, and therapists, Lexi. It's no fun being an invalid." A pained expression crossed his face. "Lots of people *are* after an accident like mine, you know. I'm very fortunate, I'm going to get a second chance."

"I've been praying for this, Todd."

"I know. A lot of people have." He looked thoughtful. "This time I've spent in the hospital has certainly made me think."

"I'm sure it has."

"I was just like every other average guy until this happened. Now I've learned to appreciate each new day. Whatever I am able to accomplish is an encouragement. The fact that I can still think rationally, and carry on a conversation with my friends is important to me now."

"As you know, when the accident first happened, all I wanted to do was give up. I didn't think there was any point in going on if there was a chance I'd never walk again."

Lexi listened intently.

"I suppose that's why I wondered if Chad hadn't been right after all . . . just end the suffering." His expression was serious, and Lexi knew he'd weighed his words for some time. "But I came to the point where I knew even the pain was good. At least I had feeling; I knew I was going to get better. I'm glad that when I was down at first, I didn't continue to listen to those accusing voices in my head. I started listening to someone else."

"Someone else?"

"God, Lexi. He's the One who pulled me through. He gave me good doctors and nurses, and therapists, and friends—friends like you and Pastor Lake to help me see how wrong I was to doubt His faithfulness." Todd started to choke on his words. "I'll always be grateful."

It was hard for Lexi to hold back her own tears. She was so thankful for his improvement. Yet, nagging doubts filled her mind. She still felt a tight knot in her stomach when she looked at him in the wheelchair.

She was afraid of how Todd might respond if he didn't continue to improve as expected. If God could give him enough faith and energy to get through the therapy and come out walking on his own, God was even more powerful than Lexi had imagined.

She was almost ashamed of her lack of faith. But here in this room full of medical equipment, special bed, walker, and wheelchair, it was still hard to imagine Todd returning to the completely normal young man he'd been before the football accident.

Someone in the doorway interrupted Lexi's solemn thoughts. A young man in a wheelchair rolled into the room. The fellow's arms and shoulders were thick and muscular, but Lexi could tell, even though he wore jeans, that the muscles of his legs were atrophied.

"What's happening?" The young man gave Todd a cheerful grin.

"I've got company. I'd like you to meet Lexi Leighton. Lexi, this is Trevor Jordan. He's in the room two doors down."

"Hi, Lexi." Trevor gave her an appraising look. "You're the best-looking thing that's come through Todd's door today, other than myself, of course," he said, jokingly.

"Trev was broadsided by a drunk driver," Todd explained.

"Bad news, huh?" Trevor shook his head. "I can still remember the night. I thought I wasn't going to make it, let alone ever drive again. But, hey, look at me now." He patted his wheelchair.

"Trevor's been taking driving lessons," Todd said with a laugh.

"Driving lessons?" Lexi didn't understand.

"Not for the chair. He just got a customized van that's fitted for his wheelchair."

"Oh, I see. That's great," Lexi tried to sound enthused.

"It's going to feel good to have some real wheels under me again. It's a little strange so far, but I'm getting the hang of it."

"That's amazing," Lexi said.

"Not really," Trevor shook his head. "Actually, it's pretty easy for me. I have good use of my hands and arms. There's another fellow taking lessons who, because he doesn't have full use of his arms, will have to drive with a specially designed lever."

"It's really something how the automobile designers can work around almost any physical disability," Todd commented.

Trevor continued to make light of their condition. "I've teased Todd here about his driving. I told him that if I ever saw him coming, I would head for the ditch, because it would probably be a lot safer than meeting him head on."

As the two discussed engine sizes and makes of automobiles, Lexi was alone with her thoughts: *These guys seem so strong and happy in spite of their problems. They sound like any two young men anywhere discussing their cars. It's hard to believe we're sitting in a rehab center.*

She wondered what it was about Chad Allan that had made him act irrationally, out of weakness and desperation. How had Todd and Trevor managed to survive, full of strength and hope?

As Lexi considered the question, Trevor turned to her and asked, "Have you tasted the food here yet?"

Lexi shook her head.

"Good. Don't. It's lousy."

"Lexi's mother's a wonderful cook," Todd said. "Maybe Lexi could smuggle some food in here for you."

"Nah. I've been ordering out. Pizza mostly. The night nurse is willing to take my money, and brings the pizza to me when it's delivered."

"How'd you manage that?" Todd wondered aloud.

"My charm and good looks, of course." Trevor grinned broadly. "Actually, the nurse has a crush on an orderly on this floor, and I'm acting as a go-between, a matchmaker-in-residence of sorts."

Lexi suppressed a chuckle. "Do you live here in Cedar River?"

"No. My home is about 150 miles away." His expression turned wistful. "I'll be glad to get home. I have a girlfriend there and my family is waiting for me."

"That's nice," Lexi said, genuinely glad to hear someone was waiting for him.

"It really is. They've been my strength through all this. I couldn't have gotten along without them and my church. People have been so kind and supportive, I can hardly even talk about it."

Lexi noticed the catch in Trevor's voice.

"When you're really down, you find out how wonderful people can be."

That was it, Lexi thought. That was the difference between Trevor and Todd, and Chad Allan. These two had a support system behind them when their tragedies occurred. They had people to love and pray for them and churches to support them.

Lexi's heart twisted with pain for Chad. He had wrongly believed that he had no one—that without Peggy he was all alone. Lexi wished there were some way to reach back in time and tell Chad that his family, his friends, the church, really had cared for him, that God loved him just the way he was. It was too late for Chad, but she could still pray for Todd, and now for his friend, Trevor.

The boys snapped Lexi out of her thoughts by

asking her to join them in a board game.

When Todd's lunch tray arrived, she stood up. "I really should go. I've been here all morning. I didn't mean to take so much of your time."

"Hey, all we've got in here is time," Trevor said. "Especially on the weekends." He glanced from Todd to Lexi. "Thanks for including me. You're both really special people."

Before Lexi could answer, Trevor wheeled himself out of the room. As he passed the nurse, he said briskly, "Steak—medium rare, hash browns and a large milk, please."

The nurse, with an ironic grin, retorted, "Macaroni and cheese, well done, hot dogs and apple juice."

Todd and Lexi could hear Trevor's groan all the way down the hall.

"You'll come back soon, won't you?" Todd asked.

"Of course."

"Good. I think I might have a surprise for you."

"A surprise? Tell me what it is. I like surprises."

"I'm not going to tell you. Then it won't be a surprise."

"When can I have it?"

"I'm not sure. Soon, I hope."

"Oooooh, you're mean." She punched his arm playfully.

Todd laughed. "You'll just have to keep coming back until I decide to give it to you. That's all."

"Well, that really doesn't sound too hard." In fact, it sounded like a wonderful idea!

———

Peggy Madison was sitting on the Leightons'

front porch when Lexi pulled into the driveway.

"Hi! Been waiting long?"

"Mom wanted me to return this cake tin, but no one's home." Peggy's eyes were cloudy and she seemed completely disinterested in the errand.

"Thank you. Do you want to come in for a while?"

Peggy made Lexi feel very uncomfortable. There was something strange about her look and the slight slur in her speech.

"No, I have to go home." Peggy stood abruptly and walked slowly toward the sidewalk.

Lexi was speechless, almost relieved that Peggy wasn't staying. She wasn't eager to talk to her friend when she was in such a strange mood. As she watched her retreat, she noticed Peggy wasn't even walking in a straight line.

When Lexi entered the quiet house, she saw the note from her mother telling her where she and Ben had gone. Lexi clutched the cake pan to her chest and leaned against the door jamb.

Why is life so turned upside-down? she wondered. *Who or what will turn things around? When will our lives be normal again?*

Chapter Eleven

"Hi, Lexi," Jennifer's voice sang across the telephone line. "Are you ready to go to the youth meeting at church tonight?"

"I'm on my way out the door. Binky's supposed to meet us at the corner. Have you called Peggy?"

"Yep," said Jennifer, the enthusiasm gone from her voice. "She said she didn't feel like going tonight."

"Hmmm, that's strange . . ." Lexi mused. "Well, I guess we'll have to go without her. Meet you at the corner?"

"Okay, see you there."

The three girls met at the designated spot minutes later. Lexi glanced at Binky and then looked down the street. "What? No Egg? Isn't he coming?"

Binky made a face and waved her hand in the air. "Oh, Egg. What a nut. He said he had to leave early because he had to go on some mysterious mission before youth group tonight."

"What kind of mission is that?" Lexi asked suspiciously. She knew all too well the crazy ideas Egg McNaughton could get into his head and the trouble he could cause.

"I have no idea. Nothing important, I'm sure. He dramatizes everything. You know that. He's probably in charge of buying paper cups for the meeting."

"How do you know his 'mission' has anything to do with the meeting?" Jennifer asked.

"Pastor Lake called. They had a big discussion on the phone. Egg made me leave the room. You know how exclusive he can be. He walked around the house afterward like he'd been elected president or something."

"We'll just have to wait and see," Lexi said philosophically. "One thing Egg *can't* do is keep a secret. We'll know what this is all about before long."

The church basement was teeming with teenagers when Jennifer, Lexi and Binky arrived.

"Big crowd tonight." Jennifer gave a low whistle. "Almost every chair is full."

"I almost forgot. That's the other thing Egg did today," Binky said. "He was on the phone all afternoon telling everyone to be sure to not miss youth group tonight."

"Good old Egg," Lexi said with a laugh. "Once he's enthused about something, there's just no stopping him."

"What an odd expression he has on his face," Jennifer said, observing Pastor Lake. He was standing at the side of the room with his arms crossed over his chest, looking at the group with a smug, satisfied smile.

"My mom would say, 'He looks like the cat that just ate the canary,'" Binky whispered.

"I wonder what he's so pleased about?"

"Maybe it's the good crowd."

"I'm sure this is the biggest youth group ever."

"Why does he keep checking his watch?"

Pastor Lake seemed restless tonight. "Do you think he and Egg have something really weird planned?" Lexi asked.

"Why would Pastor Lake ask Egg to help him with anything important?" Binky wondered, her face contorted in puzzlement. "Egg can get things muddled up faster than anyone I know."

"Oh, Binky. Give your brother some credit." Jennifer poked her in the arm.

"Well, it's true."

Lexi felt excitement snapping the air. Something was up and she couldn't imagine what. She joined Minda, who was telling a small group about her finding a super sale at the mall.

"And the white, pocket T-shirts," she was saying, "were two for the price of one! Can you believe it? I had to have half a dozen. They go with absolutely everything!"

"I don't even own six T-shirts total!" Binky hissed in Lexi's ear.

"And the shoes! Twenty-five percent off at *Flings'*. Tressa and I went wild." Minda loved to be at the center of any conversation.

Lexi didn't really mind anymore. She and Minda were getting along fine lately. She was happy to keep it that way.

Minda had just launched into another story about a cosmetic sale when the rest of the room became suddenly quiet. Lexi spun around as if on cue. All eyes were riveted on the door behind her. A small gasp escaped her lips. Egg McNaughton stood in the double doorway of the basement, his hands resting on the back of Todd Winston's wheelchair.

"Todd!" she blurted. "What are you doing here?" Lexi ran to his side.

Todd's blue eyes glowed with pleasure. "I'm the surprise I warned you about at the hospital," he said with a quiet laugh. "Well, is anyone surprised?" he said loudly.

Pandemonium broke loose as the young people rushed forward to greet him. Todd was practically buried in a mass of humanity. "Back up, back up!" Egg waved his arms frantically. "You're smothering him."

Pastor Lake smiled at the joyous reunion.

No wonder he looked so smug! Lexi thought. She could hardly believe Todd was actually with them at the church. It didn't matter that he couldn't stand or move among them. It was just so wonderful to see him here.

Pastor Lake clapped his hands. "I want you all to sit down now. I invited Todd here tonight to talk to us about what's been happening in his life since his accident. I know all of you have been very concerned, curious, and rightly so. I also know that some of you have had some fears and doubts—uncomfortable feelings about how to respond to someone who is temporarily handicapped.

"It's difficult to deal with suffering, or more particularly with the type of adjustments Todd has had to face. Since Todd is willing to share with us, I thought this would be a good time to hear firsthand about what it's like to be confined to a wheelchair."

Pastor Lake smiled warmly at Todd. "Fortunately, the good word is that the chair isn't a permanent fixture for him. But I'll let Todd tell you about that himself."

The room became even more quiet as Egg pushed Todd toward the front. For a few moments, Todd simply looked out at his friends, some of whom he hadn't seen since he was injured.

When he finally began to speak, his first words came out shaky: "I can't tell you what it means to me to be here tonight. For the first few days after my accident, I thought I'd never be seen in public again. I thought I was trapped forever." He tapped on the arm of his chair. "But now, as Pastor Lake said, things are looking more positive. I'm able to walk with a walker, and am determined to be rid of that soon. I'm very fortunate that my spinal cord wasn't severed. Because it wasn't, the prospects are good for my full recovery.

"When Pastor Lake asked me to talk to you tonight, I had a hard time deciding if I should come. It forced me to think back to the night of my accident and remember a lot of things that I've been trying to forget.

"I can still remember details about that evening—the bright lights overhead, the cheering of the fans, the smell of the fall air, the green turf beneath my feet, and most distinctly, the feeling of being on my feet one minute and the next being knocked to the ground, lying flat on my back with no feeling from my chest down. I don't have to tell you that was the most terrifying moment of my life.

"I always thought I was a tough guy, but that night I was scared. I remember the serious looks on the paramedics' faces, and my mother running onto the field, crying. I realized then that I wasn't going to get up and walk away from this one. For a while, I even wondered if I was going to die."

Todd paused, gazing at the varied expressions on the faces of each one. He took a deep breath and continued. "Those first days in the hospital I thought about a classmate of ours—Chad Allan."

No one moved. The silence in the room was almost stifling.

"When I first heard of Chad's death, I believed he'd taken the coward's way out. I remember thinking that Chad was just plain stupid to take his own life. But when *I* was lying in a hospital bed, paralyzed, with no promise that I'd ever walk again, I thought it would be better for everyone if I died, too."

Lexi gripped the arm of her chair, and the tears began to stream down her face.

"In fact, I *wished* I could die. I began to feel sorry for myself. And I was angry with Chad. I wondered why he had taken his own life when he still had use of his arms and legs. I couldn't even move!

"Then a curious thing happened to me. Your cards and letters began to arrive, the flowers and food, balloons, and crazy posters. I started to realize that people thought I was important, I was valuable, even if I couldn't walk. The negative thoughts I was having began to dissipate. Looking back, I know that someone was showing me that in spite of my injury I could still live, and I could still be happy. That someone was God himself."

Binky twisted uncomfortably in her chair, obviously moved by Todd's testimony.

"There were a lot of terribly sick and injured people in the hospital with me. As I watched some of them get well, and some of them die, I realized how precious life is. Every day is an opportunity. And even though I couldn't run, swim, play tennis or football, I knew that I still wanted to live."

"God really had to work in me, though," Todd admitted. "I was angry with everyone at first, including God. Finally, with the help of some friends . . ." Todd smiled at Lexi. ". . . I was convinced that good could come of this no matter what the outcome. I just had to trust God." Todd rapped his knuckles on the arm of his wheelchair. "I've met some really great friends in the hospital, too. Friends I will value forever."

Lexi thought of Trevor and the strong friendship she'd seen between the two.

"And I've learned to appreciate more fully some of my old friends. You came to see me. Even though I was cranky and not much for company, you didn't give up. You kept coming back, keeping me up on school activities, and telling me everything was going to be all right. I know that was hard for some of you. Visiting a hospital isn't fun, but believe me, it's even less fun being a patient in one."

Lexi glanced at Matt Windsor. His face was pale. She knew it was painful for him to listen.

"I realized I wasn't in this alone, that my friends and family were behind me, faithful and steady. Even those of you that I didn't see, I know you've prayed for me and thought of me. I really appreciate that. Don't stop now.

"You've taught me how to be a friend—how to be

there when someone's in trouble. That's the biggest and best lesson I've ever learned. Thank you."

Lexi knew there wasn't a dry eye in the room as Todd continued:

"You know, sometimes you can ignore a problem, forget about it, at least for a while. I couldn't run away from this." He hit the wheelchair with his fist. "I was trapped. I had to lie flat on my back for several days. It really made me think about myself—about my strengths and weaknesses, about what life is really about. Even though I couldn't take my body anywhere, my mind was free. I could choose to be unhappy, miserable, and bitter about my situation, or I could choose, as Chad Allan did, to end it all. I don't know how I would have done it, but the thoughts were almost as destructive as the act itself would have been. I also had the alternative to choose life—to enjoy it to the fullest. I could make the people around me happier just by my attitude. I could co-operate with the doctors and nurses and make their job easier. My small spot in the universe could be a brighter place because I was in it.

"As you can see, I chose life. With God's help, I want to do whatever I can to help others do the same. Ever since Chad's suicide I've wanted to say this, and now more than ever, I need to say it to all of you: If there is anyone here that has ever felt like your life is worthless and you'd like to end it, please *don't*. It's a bad choice. You are precious to God whether you're healthy and strong and popular, or flat on your back in a hospital bed, feeling friendless and alone. Each of us is of equal value to God. We must realize this, be convinced of it."

Todd's smile was bright and contagious. "So, little by little, I worked at being cheerful instead of crabby. I worked with the physical therapist instead of against her. I canceled the pity party I was having for myself. Once I did that, I realized that whatever God had in store for me was *okay*."

Todd paused for a long moment. "I'm very thankful that I'm regaining the use of my legs. The doctors say I should be back at school in a few weeks."

There were audible gasps, and joy was written on the faces of everyone. Minda, who was normally impassive and unflappable, was sobbing openly.

"And, I may not even need the wheelchair." He gave a mock frown. "I just want all you guys to know that using a walker doesn't mean I'll be defenseless. You'll have Egg here to deal with if you try anything funny. Right, Egg?"

Egg took a tough-guy pose behind Todd. There was an outburst of laughter.

"I guess that's about all I wanted to say." Todd grinned and nodded toward Pastor Lake. "I guess you didn't expect a sermon." His expression grew serious. "If anybody wants to talk to me, though, or cry on my shoulder, I'm available." He patted the wheelchair. "And I can't walk away from you either."

Everyone was quiet, contemplating what Todd had shared. They knew it had taken strength and conviction for him to come tonight and say the things he did. His honesty and willingness to expose his true feelings was like a healing balm for the group.

"I think Todd's given us all something very important to think about," Pastor Lake said. "So let's give some time to that when you get to your homes, and in the days ahead. Right now, I think it's appropriate that we celebrate—the healing in Todd's body, and just the fact that he's with us tonight. We'll call it a 'Welcome Back, Todd' party!"

"Let the party begin!" Jerry Randall whooped from the back of the room.

There was a sudden burst of activity, as some gathered around Todd to speak with him, and others began setting up tables in the center of the room, arranging all sorts of food and soft drinks on them. Then someone began pounding out tunes on the piano, and Tim Anders picked up his guitar to strum along.

Controlled chaos broke out. The music and laughter lasted over two hours. No one could remember when they'd enjoyed a party so much.

Todd was looking tired when the last of his friends said their goodbyes. "I think it's time I take you back to the rehab center," Pastor Lake said.

Todd smiled wearily. "It's the most excitement I've had in a long time. I hate to admit it, but I'm beat."

"That was some evening," Jennifer said after Todd and Pastor Lake had left the church. "I feel bushed."

"Want a ride home?" Jerry offered.

"I came with Lexi and Binky," Jennifer said, hesitating. "But thanks anyway."

"Go ahead," Lexi said, shooing her friend away. "Egg and Bink and I will clean up."

"Right," said Binky. "You go with Jerry."

Jennifer blushed slightly. "Okay. Thanks. I'll see you guys later."

"Egg McNaughton!" Binky said accusingly, after everyone was gone. "How could you keep a secret like Todd's coming here? I can't believe you didn't give it away!"

"It was Todd's idea," Egg said, backing away from his sister. "He wanted to surprise us all. Especially you, Lexi. Were you surprised?"

"Surprised? It's amazing I didn't faint when you walked in with Todd! But it was one of the nicest surprises I've ever had."

"Todd's always been a great guy," Egg mused. "But he's different now. A lot more thoughtful. When you talk to him, he really listens—as though every word were really important."

"I suppose when you're faced with life and death, it makes you change, either for the better or for the worse. I'm glad Todd made the right choice."

Egg and Binky exchanged glances. Lexi knew something was up.

"What's going on between you two?" she asked.

Egg leaned thoughtfully against the broom he was pushing. "Binky and I have been having some conversations about life and death, too."

"Yeah," Binky agreed. "It all started when Chad Allan committed suicide. Then Todd had his accident. I guess Egg and I were wondering if—well, maybe someone wasn't trying to tell us something."

"Someone?" Lexi asked.

Egg rolled his eyes upward. "You know, Someone with a capital S."

"Oh." Lexi nodded.

"You know, Lexi, that we aren't from a very religious home. Knowing you and Todd and coming to this youth group have been the most religious things we've ever done. It shook us up when Chad killed himself. When he lost the friendship of the person he thought he couldn't live without, he wanted to die. Neither Binky nor I agree with his choice, of course. Then Todd had his accident, and the possibility of never walking again was staring him in the face. His potential loss was so much greater than Chad's, yet he was able to keep going. I guess we'd like to know a little more about the faith that makes that happen."

"And I'd like to know a little more about Heaven," Binky said. "It sounds like a nice place, I guess, but kind of scary."

"Frankly, I'd like to know where I'm going when I die," Egg said. "I want it to be some place I can look forward to."

Pastor Lake cleared his throat. No one had heard him return, and Lexi wondered fleetingly how much he'd heard of their conversation.

"Sorry kids, I don't mean to eavesdrop, but I couldn't help hearing what you just said about life and death."

"Actually, I'm glad you came," Lexi admitted.

"You've asked some pretty powerful and important questions. The kinds of questions people struggle with all their lives."

"Really? I didn't think we were that smart," Binky said, her head down.

Pastor Lake lifted her chin affectionately. "Young lady, you underestimate yourself."

"Hey, that's the nicest thing anyone's ever said to me." Binky beamed.

"Hmmmph," Egg snorted. "I tell you that all the time."

Binky grinned. "Yeah, but I never believe you."

Pastor Lake looked at his watch. "I realize it's late, but if the two of you would like to carry on this conversation in my study, I'd be happy to."

Egg and Binky looked at Lexi. "Go ahead," she encouraged. "I'll finish sweeping and wait for you upstairs."

"Good idea," Pastor Lake said. "I'll drive you all home if you don't mind waiting."

Lexi shook her head. "Not at all. In fact, I'll even call our parents so they won't worry."

"Thanks, Lexi," Binky said, squeezing her hand.

Egg and Binky disappeared with Pastor Lake into his study.

Lexi finished the sweeping and turned out all but a single row of lights. She went upstairs and out the main doors of the church into the cool, crisp air. She stretched and took a deep breath, then laughed aloud in the darkness.

Back inside, she sat in one of the pews to think about all she had to be thankful for. She knew Egg and Binky would have lots of questions about faith, heaven and the afterlife, but she also knew Pastor Lake would have some answers. This conversation could be a turning point in their lives.

With Todd's steady improvement, and now this, Lexi had much to praise God for. There was much to be happy about tonight.

———

Todd is on the road to recovery. Egg and Binky have started attending youth group and church steadily. Life should finally be smooth once again, but not yet. Peggy is behaving very strangely. Will her life ever be normal again?

Find out in Cedar Daydreams Number 15, *Lost and Found*.

A Note From Judy

I'm glad you're reading *Cedar River Daydreams*! I hope I've given you something to think about as well as a story to entertain you. If you feel you have any of the problems that Lexi and her friends experience, I encourage you to talk with your parents, a pastor, or a trusted adult friend. There are many people who care about you!

Also, I enjoy hearing from my readers, so if you'd like to write, my address is:

Judy Baer
Bethany House Publishers
6820 Auto Club Road
Minneapolis, MN 55438

Please include an <u>addressed, stamped envelope</u> if you would like an answer. Thanks.